HOW I SURVIVED MIDDLE SCHOOL

MADAME PRESIDENT

By Nancy Krulik

SCHOLASTIC INC.

New York Toronto London Auckland Sydney
Mexico City New Delhi Hong Kong Buenos Aires

ISBN 0-439-90090-5

Published by Scholastic Inc.
SCHOLASTIC and associated logos are trademarks and/or registered trademarks of Scholastic Inc.

12 11 10 9 8 7 6 5 4 3 2 1   6 7 8 9 10 11/0

Printed in the U.S.A.   40
First printing, October 2006

What Kind of Girl Are You?

1. **There's a new boy in school and you think he's really hot. Do you**

   A. Offer to show him around, since you know how hard it is to be the new kid?

   B. Ask your best buds if they think he's cute, too? If they agree, you introduce yourself. Otherwise, forget about it.

   C. Flash him a big smile and hope he introduces himself to you?

2. **You see one of the snobbiest girls in school walk out of the bathroom with the back of her skirt stuck in her underwear. What do you do?**

   A. Start laughing so loudly that everyone looks in her direction.

   B. Let her know quietly, so she can run into the bathroom and fix things.

C. Say nothing — someone in her crowd is bound to tell her sooner or later.

3. When it's test time, what's your usual reaction?

A. You copy off the smart kid next to you — 20/20 vision's got to be good for something!

B. You're really nervous. You don't usually do well on tests.

C. You are totally confident. You studied really hard.

4. At a sleepover party, you can usually be found:

A. Sleeping. You're always the first one zzz-ing at these things.

B. Gossiping about all the kids that you didn't invite to the party.

C. Taking charge and coordinating the evening's triple-M entertainment: makeovers, manicures, and munchies.

Check your answers and add up your points.

1. A) 3 B) 1 C) 2
2. A) 1 B) 3 C) 2
3. A) 1 B) 2 C) 3
4. A) 2 B) 1 C) 3

10-12 points: Flap those wings, you social butterfly! You're the kind of girl everyone loves — confident and cool. Rock on, girl!

7-9 points: You may be shy, but it's those quiet girls who have all the surprises. Come on, gain some confidence! Let the kids at school see that amazing person you've been hiding inside.

4-6 points: You can be nice when you want to, but for some reason, you often choose to show your nastier side to others. Try making an effort to say something nice to someone today. You may just discover it makes you feel good, too.

Chapter ONE

THE FIRST PERSON I SAW when I walked into school on Monday morning was Addie Wilson. What a terrible way to start the week!

Addie was standing in front of her locker in C wing of Joyce Kilmer Middle School, with her friends, Dana and Claire. As I walked by, they started to giggle.

"Loser," Dana coughed into her hand.

"Geek," Claire added, coughing over her word as well.

"Did you see those sneakers?" Dana asked. "Nobody ever wears high-tops. How uncool."

"Jenny *is* uncool," Addie told her. "So the sneakers are perfect for her."

It's not hard to see why Addie and I aren't friends anymore.

Luckily, not everyone in my school is so obnoxious. I've got lots of friends. And none of them spend their time making fun of people.

"I see the Pops are at it again," my friend Felicia Liguori said, as she walked over to my locker with Chloe Samson, another one of my pals.

That's what we call Addie and her friends. The Pops. As

in popular. Why they're popular, I'm not quite sure. Most people think they're jerks. Of course, most people wish they could be one of them, too. I can't explain it. It's just the way it is.

"Yeah, it's makeup madness at locker 260 . . . again," I replied.

The Pops put on their makeup at Addie's locker mirror every morning. Then they wash it all off again at the end of the school day. That's because none of them are really allowed to wear makeup. If their moms saw them with all that blush, eye shadow, and lip gloss on they'd be in so much trouble.

"I don't know why Dana's laughing," Felicia said. "We got our first math test back last Friday, and she failed hers. I saw it. If I were her I'd be flipping out."

"Yeah, well, as long as her best friend Addie's by her side, Dana's happy," Chloe said. "Who needs math when you've got popularity?"

Felicia laughed at that. But I didn't. All I could think about was that Chloe had called Dana Addie's "best friend." That used to be me.

All through elementary school, Addie and I were best friends. I mean total BFF. You'd never see Addie Wilson without me – Jenny McAfee – by her side.

Then last summer I went away to summer camp, and Addie started hanging out with Dana. By the time I came back home, Addie was more interested in makeup and shopping than riding bikes around the neighborhood or building shoe-box playgrounds for my pet mice, Cody and Sam. *Those* were the kinds of things Addie and I used to do when we were together.

But we aren't friends anymore. That's because the more Addie hung out with Dana, the more Addie started to be like her. And there's just one word that can be used to describe Dana — *mean*. Now that's pretty much how I'd describe Addie, too.

"I wonder how happy Dana would be to know that Addie went to the movies with Claire and not her this weekend," Chloe said.

"Were they there by themselves?" I asked her. I knew that Addie had been bugging her mother to let her go to the movies without a grown-up. I wondered if she'd had any success. Addie's mom and my mom were friends. I figured that if Addie was allowed to go to the movies without her parents, maybe my mom would say it was okay for me to do that, too.

"Nah," Chloe said. "They wanted everyone to think they were, but I saw Claire's mom sitting two rows behind them."

Okay, so much for that.

"I've got to get to math class," Felicia said. "I'll see you on the bus after school, Jen."

"Save me a seat," I replied. Not that I had to say that. Felicia and I always sat together on the bus ride home.

"We've gotta get to English," Chloe said, as she adjusted the strap on her overalls.

I nodded, and followed Chloe down the hallway. Suddenly I spotted a huge yellow sign on the wall.

AFTER-SCHOOL CLUBS
sign-up this afternoon

Cafeteria
3:00–4:30

"Marc told me all about them," Chloe interrupted. Marc Newman was Chloe's next-door neighbor, and a seventh grader. Because he was a year older, he knew the deal about middle school. Chloe got all her information from him.

Of course, I knew about the after-school clubs, too. I'd read all about them in the handbook the school had given out at sixth grade orientation. I think I was the only kid in the school who had actually read that thing – cover to cover.

"There are all kinds of clubs," Chloe continued, as we walked down the hallway. "Like the theater club, the chess club, the art club, the Spanish club, the French club, student government . . ."

"I know. It sounds so cool," I said.

"It is," Chloe agreed. "I'm signing up for the theater club. I heard they're going to do *You're a Good Man, Charlie Brown* this year. Don't you think I'd make the perfect Lucy?"

I didn't know if Chloe could sing, dance, or act, but I did know that she had a pretty big mouth — just like the Lucy character in the *Peanuts* comics. "You're a natural," I teased.

Chloe laughed. She knew exactly what I meant. But she wasn't insulted. She knew she was loud — she was actually kind of proud of it. "So what are *you* going to sign up for?" she asked me.

"I don't know," I said. "I haven't even thought about it."

"Well, you'd better *get* thinking," Chloe warned. "The best clubs always fill up fast. Marc said that last year he wanted to be in the movie club, but he couldn't because the older kids had gotten to the cafeteria right after school and taken all the spots. He wound up having to choose between the yearbook committee and the chess club."

"Which did he choose?" I wondered.

"Yearbook," Chloe said. "He figured that way he'd at least be able to make sure there weren't any dorky pictures of him in there."

I nodded. I knew how he felt. I hated having my picture taken for just that reason.

"And besides, he doesn't play chess," Chloe continued.

Neither did I. And acting wasn't my thing, either. "I guess we'd better get to the cafeteria right after school," I said.

"Uh-huh," Chloe agreed. "I'm going to call my mom at lunch and tell her I'll be taking the late bus home today."

"Me, too," I agreed. Then I looked up at the clock. "And speaking of late . . ." I began.

Chloe got my drift. "We gotta roll!" she exclaimed, as we both took off down the hall at top speed.

By lunchtime, everyone was buzzing about the after-school clubs. It was all anyone could talk about.

"This year, I'm getting into the movie club," Marc said. "No matter what."

Marc wanted to be a movie director when he grew up. Actually, he wasn't even waiting until he grew up. He was already making a movie. It was a documentary about being in middle school.

It was so cool that Marc already knew what he wanted to be when he grew up. The last time *I* had any idea about that, I was three years old and wanted to be a fairy princess.

"I'm going to join the Spanish club," my friend Carolyn said. She flipped her long blond hair behind her shoulder and took a bite of her hot dog. "They go out for Spanish and Mexican food a lot," she added.

"That sounds like a good idea," Carolyn's identical twin sister, Marilyn, agreed. "Anything not to have to eat this slop."

"I know," I agreed, holding up my hot dog. "This tastes

like it's made of rubber. If I dropped it, I'll bet it would bounce."

Marilyn giggled. "Anyway, I'm signing up for field hockey."

"I didn't know you liked sports," I said.

"She doesn't," Carolyn interrupted. "She just likes the uniforms the girls on the team get to wear. Marilyn's much more into fashion than I am."

That made me laugh, because at that moment, the twins were wearing the exact same thing — gauzy peasant blouses. Marilyn's was yellow and Carolyn's was blue.

"What are you going to sign up for?" my friend Josh asked me.

I shrugged. "I have no idea."

"Have you talked about it with anyone else?" he wondered.

I smiled. By "anyone else" I knew he meant Felicia. He had a huge crush on her. "Well, I'm pretty sure Felicia's going to join the basketball team," I told him. "She and Rachel spent all summer playing at the community center."

"They're really good," Josh agreed. "Especially Felicia. She's promised to teach me how to make a jump shot."

"So what are you joining, Mr. Wizard?" Chloe asked. She loved to tease Josh about being smart.

"My algebra teacher asked me to sign up for the Mathletes," he replied shyly.

"I thought that was only for seventh and eighth graders," our friend Liza said.

"It is . . . usually," Josh agreed. "But since I'm already taking seventh grade algebra, I guess it's okay for me to be in it."

As Liza started talking about how she wanted to join the art club, Addie, Dana, and Claire passed by our table on their way to the bathroom. That's where all the Pops go after lunch. They hang out in there, putting on makeup, and gossiping about people. I know because I'd tried to join them at the very beginning of the school year.

What a mess that had been. They had said all kinds of mean things about me. And not when I left the room, either. Right to my face. They did stuff like that all the time.

"Check out the overalls," Dana said as she passed behind Chloe. She was pretending to whisper, but she was being loud enough for everyone to hear.

"Maybe she's going to milk the cows after school," Claire joked. "Mooo."

Addie giggled. "Too bad there's no farm club. She could be the president."

"Or the mascot," Claire added. "Moooo."

"Mooo, mooo," Dana chimed in, so loudly that a bunch of kids started staring.

Chloe just ignored them. She didn't say a word. She didn't even frown. I thought that was pretty impressive.

"Gee, I wonder what club those three are going to join?" Marilyn asked. "Maybe the moron club?"

Hmm . . . I thought about that for a minute. Addie may

have turned into a class-A jerk, but she wasn't a moron. She was actually pretty smart. I didn't know Claire very well, so I couldn't say. But Dana on the other hand . . . Well, after what Felicia had told me this morning, maybe Marilyn wasn't too far off.

Everyone at our lunch table was staring at Chloe now. Sure, she'd stayed really cool while the Pops were talking about her, but we all knew she had to be upset.

It was Liza who knew exactly what to do to cheer her up. "Check this out," she said in her soft, quiet voice. She took her hot dog out of its bun and dropped it on the floor.

The hot dog bounced! It really did. We were all hysterical. And no one laughed harder than Chloe.

I smiled happily to myself. Let the Pops spend their lunch hour staring at themselves in the bathroom mirror.

There was no way they were having more fun than we were right now!

{ Chapter } TWO

"AND HERE THEY COME, three more wild animals, fighting for survival in the jungle that is club sign-ups!" Marc said in a deep newscaster-type voice, as Chloe, Liza, and I walked into the cafeteria at the end of the school day.

I giggled as Marc shoved his video camera in our faces. Chloe let out a giant wild-animal-type roar. Liza put her hand in front of her face. She really hated being on camera. "Whoa, I thought we'd be one of the first ones," I said, looking around the room.

Obviously, I'd been wrong. It seemed like half the school was there already. Most of the kids had come right after the bell rang.

I sighed and added another rule to my growing list of things they never tell you at sixth grade orientation.

MIDDLE SCHOOL RULE # 6:
DON'T STOP AT YOUR LOCKER
BEFORE CLUB SIGN-UPS.

"You guys are going to have to fight your way to the front of the line if you're going to get anything good now," Marc noted.

He wasn't kidding. Already there were at least a half dozen tables with big CLUB FILLED signs on them.

"I'd better get moving before the theater club is full," Chloe said as she zoomed off.

"Yeah, I'd better hurry over to where the art club table is," Liza said, glancing across the room. The line was already snaking around the corner.

As Liza left, Marc shook his head. "She's a seventh grader. She should have known better than to get here so late. After last year, I wasn't taking any chances."

"Did you get into the movie club?" I asked him.

Marc nodded. "I was one of the first ones here. I asked to go to the nurse in the middle of my last period class. I stopped there, got my cough drop, and ran to the cafeteria."

I giggled. That was a big joke at our school. No matter what you had wrong with you, the nurse would give you a cough drop. Sore throat — cough drop. Headache — cough drop. Broken leg — cough drop. That was pretty much all she had in there.

"So what did you decide on?" Marc asked me.

"I haven't," I admitted. "There are so many choices. I don't know. . . ."

Before I could finish my sentence, Liza reappeared at my side. Her eyes had welled up with tears. "I was too late. I got closed out of the art club . . . again," she told us quietly.

Marc pulled out his camera and started filming. "Disappointment runs rampant during club sign-ups," he said into the microphone.

"Turn that off," I told him. Sometimes boys can be so insensitive.

"Sorry," he replied sheepishly as he lowered the camera.

"There are other clubs," I told Liza gently.

Liza shook her head. "Drawing and painting are the only things I'm good at."

"Maybe you're good at something else and you just don't know it yet," I suggested. "You could find out you're great at chess or field hockey or cooking. . . ."

Liza shook her head. "Forget it," she said. "I'll just ask my mom if I can take an art class at the community center."

But Liza wanted to be in an after-school club. I could tell. There had to be something left for her.

I looked around the room. Suddenly I spotted Chloe, happily signing her name to a club list. "That's it!" I shouted out. "Liza, you're going to join the theater club."

"What?" Liza looked at me as though I had three heads. So did Marc.

I smiled, knowing what they were thinking. Shy Liza in a play? No way! But that wasn't what I had in mind at all. "You can draw and paint scenery for the show," I told her. "I'm sure they need a lot of people to do that. It would still be art. Just a different kind."

Liza thought about that for a minute. "I don't know . . ." she began.

"Come on, Liza," Marc urged. "It'll be fun. Jenny's right. They need someone who can really draw. And you can draw."

"I guess," she said slowly.

"I'll walk you over," I told her.

"But don't *you* want to get in a line for something?" Liza asked me.

I shrugged. "I still don't know what club I want to be in."

"It's okay. You just pick something and sign up," Liza said. "I can go over by myself."

I smiled as I watched her go. Liza would be really happy working on the sets for the play. Now the question was, what would *I* be happy doing?

I didn't even have time to think about that before Felicia and Rachel Schumacher came running over to me. They looked really upset.

"Jenny, please tell me you haven't signed up for anything yet," Rachel exclaimed.

I shook my head. "No. I still haven't de —"

"Oh, thank goodness!" Felicia exclaimed. "This is great!"

"It's great that I don't know what club I want to be in?"

"You've got to go sign up for student government," Felicia said, practically begging.

"What?" I asked. Student government? That hadn't even been on my short list. (Not that I really *had* a short list.) "Me? Why?"

"Because Addie just decided to run for sixth grade

president," Rachel explained. "And so far no one's running against her."

"That means Addie could be our representative in student council," Felicia added. "And no Pop is going to represent me!"

"I'm sure someone else will sign up to run," I told them.

"Not someone who will win," Felicia argued. "You have lots of friends. You could beat her."

I smiled to myself. *You have lots of friends.* That sounded really nice. Like I was popular or something. Not in a Pops way, of course. But popular just the same.

"I don't know," I said. "Being class president is a big deal. I don't think I want to do something that huge."

"Well, somebody has to," Rachel said. "Think about it. Addie's already walking around like she's queen of the school. If she wins this . . ."

Rachel had a point. Addie would be completely unbearable if she won. But I wasn't sure I was the one to take her on. "What about one of you two?" I suggested.

"We're already signed up for basketball," Rachel said. "That means after-school practice three days a week."

"That's a lot of practicing," I said.

"It's cool. We love playing hoops," Felicia told me.

"And speaking of basketball, do you know why you can't play hoops with pigs?" Rachel asked.

I smiled. I knew just what was coming — another one of Rachel's bad jokes. "Why?" I asked her.

"Because they *hog* the ball," Rachel joked.

Ouch.

"Can we get back to the election?" Felicia urged, turning back toward me. "Jenny, you gotta run. You're our only hope."

"What about Josh?" I asked. "He's a sixth grader, and he's really smart. You should be smart if you're going to be class president."

"He's in the Mathletes club, remember?" Felicia said. "And besides, you're smart, too. Not as smart as Josh, but . . ."

I sighed. No one was as smart as Josh. At least not as far as Felicia was concerned.

"Come on," Rachel urged. "Just put your name on the list. Then you can think about it tonight. If you decide not to do it, you can always cross it off."

I shrugged. It's not like I'd put my name on any other list. Judging by all the FILLED signs that were popping up around the cafeteria, I'd run out of options, anyway.

"All right, I'll sign up," I said finally. "But I'm not saying I'll actually run."

My heart was racing as I got off the late bus and headed toward my house. Me? President of the sixth grade? Impossible. Especially if Addie was running. She was a Pop. *Maybe even the poppest sixth grade Pop of all.* I didn't have a chance against her.

Or did I? There really weren't that many Pops in the

sixth grade. And there were a whole lot of the rest of us. If I could get those people to vote for me . . .

But would they?

And if they didn't, and Addie won, would she ever let me forget that I'd tried to beat her?

Talk about a tough decision. I was going to need some help with this one. And since I already knew what all my friends wanted me to do – you should have heard Chloe squeal when Felicia told her I'd signed up – I would have to go to someone who didn't have any opinion at all. Someone who could help me decide this scientifically.

I would have to ask for help from my computer. Well, actually a website on my computer called middleschool-survival.com. That site is awesome. It's got all kinds of quizzes and advice columns just for middle-schoolers. I knew I could find a quiz on there that would tell me exactly what to do.

I raced over to the computer and quickly typed in the Web site. I clicked on the link for quizzes and almost immediately a whole list appeared on the screen. I scanned down past quizzes like *Are You Really What You Eat?*, *Is He Heinous or Harmless?*, and *Are You a Diva or a Dud?*, until I found just the one I needed.

Were You Born to Lead?

1. **It's Saturday afternoon, and you're bored out of your skull. Do you**

   A. Curl up on the couch and watch a marathon of MTV's *My Super Sweet 16*?
   B. Send a text message to your friends to see if they have something planned . . . and if you can tag along?
   C. Round up your friends for an afternoon hike? Nature is calling!

That was easy. My answer was definitely C. A few weeks ago, when school had just started, I probably would have checked A or B, because I would have been too shy to call any of my new friends and suggest a plan. But now I felt totally comfortable with them.

2. **Dinner's over. The dishes are piled in the sink. What's your game plan?**

   A. Call a friend and hope your mom will be too nice to interrupt your call to ask you to do the dishes.
   B. Hurry upstairs and start your homework, successfully avoiding your chores.

C. Hop to it and immediately start rinsing off the grease and grime.

Okay, if I were being completely honest, I'd have to click B here. I could never just lie around and watch my mom and dad do all the work, but I wouldn't volunteer for chores, either. At least doing my homework would be a good thing, right?

3. It's oral report time in English class! What's your plan of action?

A. Sink down low in your chair and hope the teacher doesn't notice you.

B. Make sure you've got your report out and ready just in case you get called on.

C. Volunteer to go first — better to get it over with than to have the whole thing hanging over your head.

I guess it was another B for me. I always have my work ready to go, but I don't usually volunteer to go first for anything.

4. There's a school dance coming. Do you

A. Start planning what you're going to wear, and let others plan the dance.

B. Wait to see if a planning committee forms, and then sign up to help.

C. Start your own planning committee, so you can be sure it'll be the hottest night of the year.

I wasn't sure what to click for this one. The only school dance we'd had was planned by the faculty, since it was held the second week of school. But it sounded like an excellent idea to start a planning committee with my friends, because then we could make sure we had a good time. But I didn't know about starting the committee. Was that the kind of thing sixth graders did? After thinking about it for a while, I clicked B. It was sort of a compromise.

5. **Your study group is ready to take a chow break. The trouble is, two of you are arguing over whether to go with pepperoni or mushrooms on the pizza. How do you handle this?**

A. Ignore the fighting duo. You hate getting in the middle of things, and besides, you'll eat anything.

B. Tell your friends you think arguing over pizza is totally ridiculous and suggest you get half with pepperoni and half with mushrooms.

C. Suggest that everyone in the study group vote for his or her favorite. The topping with the most votes wins.

Definitely C. I hate being around people who are fighting. And I'll do just about anything to stop it. The voting thing worked for me.

That was the last question. I clicked the SUBMIT button and held my breath as I waited for the computer to decide my future.

You have chosen three B's and two C's.
How Do You Measure Up?

If you answered mostly A's, you tend to shy away from the spotlight. Leading's not your thing. You're also not a big joiner.

It's okay to do things on your own, but you might want to give getting involved a shot. You'd be surprised how much fun it can be!

If you answered mostly B's, you are a team player. You may not be a natural-born leader, but you're not one to shirk responsibility, either. Don't be surprised if your friends come to you for a helping hand.

If you answered mostly C's, baby you were born to lead!

Okay, so now what was I supposed to do? I was stuck somewhere between being a team player and a natural-born leader.

Maybe that meant I shouldn't run for president. Maybe I should just sign up to be on a bunch of committees during the year. That way I could help out, but I wouldn't have to be in charge.

Still, the website did say that my friends would come looking for me to lend a helping hand. And that's exactly what they'd done. They'd asked me to stop Addie from becoming the president of our grade.

How could I let them down?

Chapter THREE

"OKAY, SO IT'S SETTLED. Liza and I will make the posters. Felicia's going to help you with the speech, and Josh is going to . . ." Chloe stopped for a minute. "Josh, what *are* you going to do?"

Everyone at our lunch table turned toward Josh. It was the day after I'd signed up to run in the election, and already Chloe had named herself my campaign manager.

"I could set up a 'Vote for Jenny' website," Josh suggested. "I'm good with computers."

"I could videotape you talking about the issues," Marc volunteered, holding up his camera, "and then feed the video into the website."

The issues. Yikes. I hadn't thought about that. I was going to have to come up with a platform — my feelings on how to make the school a better place. I didn't have any feelings about that. I'd only been at this school a few weeks.

"I wonder what issues Addie's going to talk about in *her* campaign," I said.

"Probably bigger mirrors in the bathrooms," Chloe joked.

I giggled. Addie did spend a lot of time looking at herself these days.

"More like how to improve the cafeteria's dessert menu," Liza said. "Looks like she's already handing out her own treats." Liza pointed across the room. Addie and Dana were passing out little bags of candy.

Eventually, Dana made her way over to our side of the cafeteria. As she passed our table, she glared at Chloe and me. She didn't give us any candy, either. In fact, the only person at our table she did give candy to was Josh.

"What's that about?" Chloe demanded. "Are you some sort of double agent spying for the other side?"

Josh looked at her. "No. I don't know why she gave me this. Honest."

"She's probably trying to divide and conquer," Marilyn suggested.

"Yeah. Maybe she's hoping she can get us so mad at Josh that we won't focus on the campaign," Carolyn added.

"But we'll never be divided," Marilyn swore.

"Yeah, we'll stick together," Carolyn vowed.

I looked down at the bag of candy on Josh's tray. There were four chocolate kisses in the bag. It was sealed with a sticker that read:

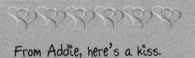

From Addie, here's a kiss.
Vote for her. She can't miss.

"I can't believe she's already campaigning," I groaned. "We just signed up for the election yesterday."

"It's okay," Chloe said. "We're pacing ourselves." She thought for a moment. "But we'd better come up with something for lunchtime tomorrow."

"I can't believe we only have one week. Next Monday is the campaign speech assembly and then everyone votes on Tuesday," I said nervously.

"I know," Chloe nodded. "We've got to get thinking. What kinds of snacks can we give out?"

"How about if we bake cookies?" Carolyn suggested.

"Yeah, everyone loves cookies," Marilyn agreed.

"But are you guys allowed to help me?" I asked the twins, glancing at Liza and Marc, too. "I mean, these are the sixth grade elections."

"There are no rules about that," Marc said. "You can help anyone you want. It's a free country."

Chloe looked over toward where Addie was handing out her candy treats. "Not if Addie gets elected. Then it'll be free only if you're a Pop. The rest of us will have to do what Addie says. That's what we've gotta stop." She paused for a moment. "Hey, that's a pretty good campaign slogan: Stop the Pop . . . Before She Stops You!"

Stop the Pop. Yeah. I liked that.

My house turned into election central after school that day. Liza, Felicia, Rachel, and Chloe were at my dining room table making signs. Josh and Marc were in the living room, working on the website on Josh's laptop. Marilyn, Carolyn, and I were in the kitchen, getting ready to bake cookies.

"Do you guys know a good recipe for cookies?" I asked the twins.

They both shook their heads. "At our house it's slice and bake," Carolyn said.

"Yeah. Our mom's not big on making stuff from scratch," Marilyn added.

"Well, we can't just buy cookies," I said. "These have to be homemade and delicious. It's the only way our campaign snack will be better than Addie's. I mean, what did she do? Buy a few candies and shove them into bags?"

"Maybe your mom has a good recipe," Marilyn said.

"I doubt it. We don't bake much around here, either," I admitted.

"We could check the computer," Carolyn suggested.

The computer! That was it! "I know just the site," I said.

Sure enough, middleschoolsurvival.com had a whole recipe section. "Let's see," I said, looking at the list. "Oh, yuck. Amazing Artichoke Hearts . . ."

"Ugh," Chloe shouted from the other room. "We don't want to make everyone throw up."

Agreed. "Marvelous Milk Shakes . . ." I continued, scanning all the recipes on the site.

"Too hard to bring to school," Felicia warned.

"But easy to make," Rachel told her. "All you gotta do

to make a milk shake is sneak up behind a cow and yell boo!" Rachel giggled. "Get it?"

"That was awful," Felicia groaned.

I smiled and changed the subject from bad jokes back to cookies. "Oh, here we go," I said when I came across some cookie recipes.

The twins and I scanned the list.

"Mmm . . . chocolate chip," I noted, looking at one recipe.

Marilyn shook her head. "Chocolate equals zits," she pointed out.

"You don't want kids blaming their lousy skin on you," Carolyn warned.

"How about sugar cookies?" I suggested, glancing down the list of recipes. "Everyone loves them."

"That's true," Marilyn agreed.

"Print it out," Carolyn told me.

With two clicks of the mouse, I did just that.

A few minutes after Marilyn, Carolyn, and I put the first batch of cookies in the oven, I heard Josh's cell phone ring.

He flipped it open. "Hello?" he said. He paused while the person on the other end said something, and then he asked, "Why are you calling me? How'd you get this number?"

Okay, that sounded a little mysterious. I couldn't help but eavesdrop.

"Um . . . well . . . I don't know," Josh stammered. "I

Yummy in the Tummy
Sugar Cookies

INGREDIENTS:
$1/2$ cup butter, softened
$1/2$ cup margarine, softened
1 egg
1 teaspoon orange extract
2 cups white sugar
2 $1/2$ cups self-rising flour
Optional: Sprinkles or small candies

YOU'LL ALSO NEED:
Large mixing bowl
An electric mixer
Measuring cup
Baking sheet
Spatula

DIRECTIONS:
1. Preheat oven to 350 degrees F.
2. Beat all ingredients in the mixing bowl, except self-rising flour, with an electric mixer until fluffy.
3. Add self-rising flour and mix well.
4. Shape dough into balls, coat in sprinkles or favorite toppings, and flatten on an ungreased cookie sheet.
5. Bake for 5 to 8 minutes until cookies are light golden brown.

Makes 24 cookies.

mean. Why me?" He listened to the person on the other end and then said, "Look, I can't talk about this right now. I'm . . . uh . . . well, I'm busy. We can talk about this tonight."

There was complete silence as he hung up the phone. It was kind of obvious that we'd all been listening in on his conversation.

"That, uh, that was my cousin," he said quickly.

I looked across the kitchen and into the dining room. Chloe and I made eye contact. She shook her head. I knew exactly what she meant. That wasn't a cousin kind of conversation. It was too suspicious.

I glanced over at Felicia to see if she had noticed how weird Josh had sounded on the phone. But she was happily putting glitter on a poster. She didn't seem to think there was anything strange about the call.

"Oh, no! Pull out those cookies, fast!" Carolyn shouted to me.

"They're gonna burn," Marilyn screamed out.

The sound of their voices brought my attention back to the baking. Quickly, I grabbed two pot holders, and pulled out the sheet of cookies.

Phew. I'd gotten to them just in time.

When I went to bed that night, there were 120 little bags of cookies in a box in my living room. Every one of them was sealed with a sticker that said, "Be a Smart

Cookie — Vote for Jenny!" Chloe had come up with that one, too. She sure was good with slogans.

I was so tired that I practically fell asleep before my head hit the pillow. And all night long I dreamed of round sugar cookies — except these cookies all had Addie's face on them. And every Addie-faced cookie was laughing at me!

I'd only been a candidate for 24 hours, and already the campaign was stressing me out.

Felicia and I giggled as we stared at the poster that Addie and her friends had posted in C wing the next morning. There was a photo of Addie and below it it read, "Vote for Addie. She's Rad-die."

"Rad-die?" Felicia chuckled. "Give me a break."

"That is pretty bad," I agreed.

Just then Chloe came rushing over to us. She was carrying a pile of posters and some masking tape. "Come on, you guys, start putting these up," she said, plopping the posters into our arms. She was in total campaign-manager mode. "This election isn't going to win itself, you know."

As I placed my poster on the wall across from Addie's, I frowned. The photograph on Addie's poster was of Addie in a long black dress, with her blond hair pulled back in a tight bun. She looked like a model.

I was wearing a pink-and-green polo shirt and jeans in my photo. My hair was in a ponytail. I didn't look like a dork or anything. I just didn't look very cool. At least not the way Addie did.

"I look like a baby in that picture," I groaned.

"No, you don't," Felicia said. "You look eleven."

"But I don't *want* to look eleven," I insisted. "Check out Addie's poster. She looks like a teenager."

"Addie and Dana are the only ones in the whole grade who look like that," Chloe pointed out. "Everyone else is more like you. Trust me. It's perfect. People will relate to this picture. It shows you're one of them."

I shrugged. Chloe sounded so sure of herself. But I wasn't quite as certain. I still wished I could look more like Addie. And I bet other people did, too.

Would that make them vote for her?

{ Chapter } FOUR

"HI, I'M JENNY MCAFEE. I'm in a few of your classes. I hope you'll vote for me for sixth grade class president," I said to two girls I recognized from my Spanish and math classes, as I handed them cookies. That was how I was spending my lunch period – handing out cookies and introducing myself to people. Chloe called it a "meet-and-greet opportunity."

I don't know where she gets this stuff.

"Mmm . . . cookies," Celina, one of the girls, remarked.

"Homemade," I assured her. "They're delicious."

"Oh, yum," her friend Emily said, taking a bite. "I love sugar cookies."

"These are totally better than those candies Addie gave out yesterday," Celina said. "I'm not a big chocolate eater."

"It gives you zits," Emily added.

I smiled. Marilyn and Carolyn had been right.

"I bet Addie's really surprised someone had the guts to run against her," Emily continued.

"I have no idea," I told her. "But I do know that I have some ideas about how to make this school great. And I want everyone to hear them. That's why I'm running."

Wow. I was really starting to sound like a politician.

"Well, I think you're really brave. Addie can be pretty mean when she wants to be," Emily remarked.

I frowned slightly. No one knew that better than I did.

"Mmmm," Celina sighed, as she licked the cookie crumbs from her fingers. "That was yummy. Can I have some more?"

Before I could hand her a second bag of cookie, Chloe grabbed me by the arm. "Sorry, guys, but I have to talk to the future Madame President right away."

"Oh, okay," Emily said as Chloe dragged me off. "Thanks again, Jenny."

"What's so important?" I asked, as Chloe and I moved away from Celina and Emily.

"You can't give out seconds on the cookies," Chloe said. "You have to give everyone just one. Otherwise it'll look like you're playing favorites with people. You can't make it look like you're the kind of person who would treat some people better than others."

"But she asked for more and —" I began.

"Look, Jenny, we're trying to show that Addie will run the school only for the Pops. *You're* the candidate who will represent everyone," Chloe explained.

"I doubt the Pops want me to represent them," I corrected her.

"Yeah, but there aren't that many of them. And besides, they're all gonna vote for Addie. We're campaigning for the other —" Chloe stopped mid-sentence and stared at the doorway in the front of the cafeteria. "What's going on over there?" she asked.

I followed her glance. Whoa! Josh was standing by the door, talking to Dana. I watched in amazement as she wrote something on a slip of paper and handed it to him. He nodded and then tucked it in his jeans pocket.

"Josh and Dana?" Chloe asked. "Since when?"

I shook my head. "Nah. It can't be. Josh likes Felicia. Everyone knows that."

"It sure doesn't look that way," Chloe said. "Look at how close she's standing to him. And he's not backing away."

"Maybe she's whispering and he has to stand that close to hear what she's saying," I suggested.

"What could Dana have to say to Josh that would be so interesting he'd want to hear it?" Chloe countered. "Unless . . ."

"Unless what?" I asked.

"Unless *he's* the one who's doing the whispering," Chloe said.

"Huh?"

"Maybe he's actually on Addie's side in this election," Chloe continued. "Maybe he's a double agent."

"Oh, come on," I said. "Josh? Spying for the Pops? Give me a break."

"Dana did give him that bag of candy yesterday," Chloe pointed out. "And he got that weird phone call."

"Yeah, but if he was a spy, wouldn't she be pretending she *didn't* like him?" I asked. "This is too obvious. Spies are supposed to be sneaky."

"Maybe," Chloe said. "But I wouldn't talk about our campaign secrets in front of him . . . just in case."

"What campaign secrets?" I asked her.

"Well, if we get any, we're not going to share them with Josh," Chloe told me. Then she pushed me back into the lunchroom. "Come on, we still have a lot of cookies to give out. You're going to win this election, with or without Josh's help."

At the end of the school day, I was walking happily through C wing, minding my own business, when Addie and Dana leaped out from behind a classroom door and blocked my path.

"You're such a baby, Jenny," Addie shouted at me.

"What are you talking about?" I asked her.

"You know exactly what I'm talking about," Addie said. "My posters."

"What about them?"

Addie moved aside so I could see the wall. There was her photograph, the one with her in the black dress and the bun in her hair. But someone had drawn a mustache and beard on her face with a black marker. The words had been changed, too. Now they read: *Don't* Vote for Addie. She's *a Bad*-die!

I choked back a laugh.

"It's not funny," Dana said. "We worked hard on those posters."

"I'm sure you did," I told her. "And I didn't do anything to them."

"Oh, come on, Jenny. You're jealous of how good I look in my picture," Addie insisted. "That's why you ruined it."

"You're so conceited," I replied. "I'm not jealous of you."

Okay, so maybe I was a little jealous of Addie. But I wasn't about to tell her that.

"Yeah, well, if you didn't do it, one of your stupid friends must have," Addie insisted.

"They're not stupid. And they wouldn't do something like this, either," I defended them. "Anyone could have drawn on your poster, Addie."

Dana stepped a little closer to me — too close.

But just then, Marc, Chloe, and Felicia walked up behind me. Suddenly it was four of us against two of them. Apparently Dana didn't like those odds, because she took a step back.

MIDDLE SCHOOL RULE # 7:
THERE'S SAFETY IN NUMBERS.

"Which one of you losers ruined Addie's poster?" Dana demanded.

"You're the only loser I see around here," Marc shot back. "So it must have been you."

"I'm not a loser," Dana told him. "I'm on Addie's team. *The winning team.*"

"Don't count on it," Felicia said.

"You guys had better watch out," Addie warned us.

"No, *you'd* better watch out," Chloe replied. "We're gonna beat you on election day."

Addie and Dana started to laugh. "Yeah, like that'll ever happen."

"We've got a few tricks up our sleeves," Chloe told them.

"Oh, so do we," Dana assured her. "Trust me."

"Is that a threat?" Marc demanded.

Addie shook her head. Her eyes grew small and mean. "No. It's a promise," she said.

I didn't like the sound of that.

As Dana and Addie walked away, I turned to Chloe. "What tricks?" I asked her.

Chloe shrugged. "I don't know. I just wanted to scare them."

"Well, we'd better come up with something," Felicia said. "I don't trust Dana and Addie. They fight dirty."

Suddenly I felt a nervous twinge in my stomach. My mind switched back to that whole Josh and Dana in the cafeteria thing. What if that was the trick Addie had been talking about?

"Hey, don't worry," Marc assured me. "We'll come up with something. You're gonna win. You'll see."

I sure hoped he was right.

{Chapter FIVE}

"OKAY, SO HERE ARE the points you want to make," Felicia said as she and Chloe sat down beside me underneath the tree in my front yard late that afternoon. "Even though sixth graders are the youngest in the school, our voice really counts, because the changes that are made this year are the ones we'll have to live with for the next three years."

"Right. Then go into the plans you have. Like to put a jukebox in the cafeteria as a way to raise money," Chloe added.

"And field days," Felicia continued.

"Oh, yeah. Definitely don't forget field days," Chloe agreed. "When the whole school goes to the park instead of classes and has races and plays games and things. It's a great way to get to know each other and boost school spirit."

"That's an important one," Felicia agreed. "Who *wouldn't* vote for someone who can get everyone out of classes for a day?"

"I don't think the principal will go for that," I said.

"She doesn't have to," Chloe explained. "You're just saying that's what you want. You'll bring it up at student council meetings. You're not actually promising you'll make it happen."

"But if we know it won't . . ." I began.

"We *don't* know," Chloe said. "The principal might think it's a great idea. *We* all do."

"That's true," I said slowly. I looked up at Marc. "Let's go," I said.

"All right," he said, aiming his digital video camera in my direction. "And . . . action!"

It took me about three tries to get the speech just right, but finally, everyone was happy with what I said on camera.

"Okay, let's bring the camera inside so we can download this," Felicia said cheerfully. "Josh must have the website almost up and running by now. I don't know how he does it. He's so smart."

"Let's hope he doesn't ou*t*smart us," Chloe murmured to me.

"What?" Felicia asked.

"Nothing," I assured her. "Come on, let's get inside and give this to him right away. I can't wait to see the website and those other posters Liza's making."

"Liza's an amazing artist," Chloe told me. "She's already working on some scenery designs for *You're a Good Man, Charlie Brown.* They're awesome."

"When are the auditions?" I asked her.

"Next Friday. Three days after the election. So I have plenty of time to get ready," she answered.

Wow. It was hard to believe the elections were next Tuesday.

"Okay, we're here," Marc called out as we headed for the living room. "You ready for the video yet, Josh?"

"Yeah, in a minute." He moved aside so we could see the screen on his laptop. "Here, check out what I've done so far."

Josh clicked the mouse, and my picture appeared on the screen. Underneath my face it said: JENNY MCAFEE, OF THE PEOPLE, FOR THE PEOPLE." Then a balloon came on the screen with a picture of Addie on it. A giant sewing needle suddenly appeared, popping the balloon. The caption read: POP THE POP. VOTE FOR JENNY.

"That's hilarious, Josh," Felicia laughed. "I love that whole balloon thing."

Marc handed Josh his camera and a connecting cable. "Here you go," he said. "The video's all ready for you to download."

Josh nodded, and connected the cable to the computer and the camera. He waited for the video icon to appear on the screen, then he double-clicked the mouse and waited.

And waited. And waited.

But nothing happened. At least not at first. Then, suddenly, the computer shut down.

"Oh, man. It crashed," Josh said. He pushed a few buttons, and turned the computer on again.

"It's all right, just pull up the file and try again," Felicia urged him.

Josh nodded and began searching. But after a few moments he frowned and said, "It's not here."

"What do you mean it's not there?" Chloe demanded.

"I mean I can't find the file. It's missing," Josh said.

"The file just can't be missing," Marc insisted.

"I know," Josh said. "It's probably just in a different folder or something. It's going to take some time, but I'll find it," he assured me, as he shut down the computer.

"What are you doing?" Chloe demanded.

"I gotta go," Josh told her.

"But the website . . ." I mumbled.

"Don't worry. I'll find it," Josh promised again.

"You have to fix it now," Chloe insisted. "There are only six days until the election. Kids have to be able to go on the site right away."

"And I've already put the address on the posters," Liza told him. She pointed to the bottom of the glittery poster she was working on.

"Come on, man, just try and find it now," Marc urged.

"I'm sorry, but I gotta do something important," Josh said.

"What's more important than this?" Chloe demanded.

Josh bit his lip and looked down at the floor. "I'll call you guys later," he said as he left.

"See, I told you," Chloe said to me the minute we heard the front door close behind him.

"Told you what?" Felicia asked suspiciously.

I sighed. "Chloe thinks Josh is a spy for Addie's side."

"That's ridiculous!" Felicia exclaimed. "How could you say that about him?"

"Look, everyone knows you like Josh, so I can't expect you to be objective about this," Chloe told her. "But first there was the candy thing, and then that whole freaky conversation he was having with Dana, and now this –"

"What candy thing? What freaky conversation with Dana?" Felicia asked nervously.

"It was nothing," I told her.

"Some nothing," Chloe argued. "First Dana gives him a bag of candy –"

"It was campaign candy," I corrected her. "She gave it to lots of people."

"Not at our table," Marc pointed out.

"Exactly," Chloe said. "And let's not forget about the mystery phone call he got yesterday. Then at lunch today, there he was, talking to Dana. And she gave him that note, and he put it in his pocket. . . ."

Felicia stared at Liza and me. "Did you guys see this, too?"

Liza shook her head. "I didn't. But Chloe told me about it."

"Jenny?" Felicia asked.

I nodded slowly. "I saw them. But, Felicia, we don't know what he was talking about with her."

"I'll bet he's with Addie and Dana right now," Chloe insisted. "He's probably telling them all about our website."

"Our *crashed* website . . ." Marc said.

"I'm just glad he didn't get a chance to download the video," Chloe said. "We don't want them to know our campaign platform."

"I don't believe you guys!" Felicia shouted. "Josh is our friend. You can't really believe he'd do this."

"Oh, yes I can," Chloe said. "And you'd better believe it, too."

I could see tears forming in Felicia's eyes. "I'm going home!" She glared at Chloe and then stormed off.

I sighed, remembering what Marilyn had said about Dana trying to divide and conquer us by giving Josh candy.

That was definitely what was happening. Except we didn't need Dana's help. We were doing it all by ourselves.

That night, Felicia called me. I could hear in her voice that she'd been crying.

"You don't really believe all that stuff Chloe was saying about Josh, do you?" she asked me.

"I don't want to think one of my best friends is a spy," I said. "But you gotta admit . . ."

"No, I don't. I don't have to admit anything!" Felicia insisted. She paused for a minute. "Do you think Josh likes Dana now?" she asked quietly.

"I don't know," I told her honestly. "I'm not really good when it comes to stuff like that."

"Well, how am I supposed to know?" Felicia asked.

I thought about that for a minute. "Remember when we did that quiz on the computer together at the beginning of school?" I asked her.

"You mean the one that told you if a boy likes you or not?" Felicia recalled.

"Uh-huh," I said. "Maybe there's another quiz to see if he *still* likes you."

"Sounds good," Felicia said hopefully.

"Hold on. I'll see if I can find one," I said, booting up my computer and going directly to www.middleschool survival.com. "Here it is. . . ."

Is He Still Into You?

True or False: Lately you've discovered that he's being very secretive.

"I don't think Josh is secretive," Felicia said.

I sighed. It was going to be hard to get Felicia to answer these questions honestly. "How about today when he wouldn't tell us where he had to go? Or yesterday, when he wouldn't tell us who called him?"

"He said it was his cousin on the phone, remember?" Felicia insisted.

"Come on, Felicia," I said. "Is that how you talk to your cousin?"

"Okay," Felicia admitted finally. "Check true."

True or false: He's stopped using your pet name.

"That's definitely false," Felicia said.

"It is?" I asked.

"He never had a pet name for me," Felicia explained. "So he couldn't stop using it."

I guess I had to give her that one. I clicked on the FALSE button.

True or false: Lately you've seen him hanging around with other girls.

"I haven't," Felicia said. "Except for you, Liza, and the twins. And that's nothing new. You guys always have lunch together."

"What about that whole thing with Dana?" I pointed out. I didn't want to be cruel. But you can't get a good answer from a computer quiz if you don't answer the questions honestly.

"I didn't see that. Chloe did. And I don't believe anything I don't see with my own eyes."

Well, the questions did say "Lately *you've* seen him . . ." So I had to click FALSE.

True or false: He's stopped paying you compliments.

"False. False. Totally false!" Felicia said excitedly. "Just this morning he told me that I was the best basketball player in the school. Girl or boy. That's a huge compliment. You have to put false this time, Jenny."

"Okay, okay," I said. "False it is." I clicked the button, and then waited. A few seconds later, the results popped up on the screen.

You answered one true and three false.

Mostly true: Sorry, but it's time to say bye-bye to your guy. He's got his sights set on someone else.

Mostly false: Don't worry, this guy's still totally into you.

"Phew," Felicia said, taking a deep breath. "That was a close one. But now that we've proved Josh still likes me, that means he could never be a spy."

"Mmm-hmm," I said, trying hard to sound as positive as Felicia did. But I wasn't sure at all. There was definitely something weird about how Josh was acting. And no computer quiz could convince me differently.

Chapter Six

MY CELL PHONE BEGAN TO RING even before my alarm clock went off the following morning. I rolled over and answered groggily.

"Hello?"

"I told you Josh was on our side," the voice on the other end said excitedly.

"Hi, Felicia. What are you talking about?"

"The website. It's up and running. And it's great."

I sat up in bed. This was pretty exciting. I'd never had my own website before. "I can't believe you got up so early just to check," I told Felicia.

"I didn't. Josh called me to tell me," she explained. "That's how I woke up."

I smiled. Felicia probably didn't mind being woken up by a call from Josh.

"Go take a look," Felicia said excitedly. "I'm gonna call Chloe and tell her she was wrong about Josh."

I laughed. I didn't know which Felicia was more excited about — that Chloe was wrong, or that the website was up and running. Probably both.

I hung up the phone and ran downstairs to the

computer. As soon as the website loaded, the video of me speaking popped up.

"Hi, I'm Jenny McAfee. And I'm running for sixth grade president . . ."

Did you ever notice how different you sound when you hear a recording of your voice? You spend your whole life thinking you sound one way, and then you hear yourself in a recording, and it's a lot squeakier. I guess that's why so many people think they can sing really well, when they can't even carry a tune.

But even though my voice was kind of high-pitched, I thought it still sounded pretty nice. And the video *looked* really professional. Marc had done a great job filming me as I talked. I didn't look like a dork at all. I sounded like I knew what I was talking about — thanks to all that coaching from Felicia and Chloe.

Watching myself on the screen, I was kind of amazed. I had to admit, I actually looked presidential. Maybe I could do this after all.

By the time I got to school in the morning, Liza and Rachel had already placed posters with my new campaign website address all over the halls. They were really nice posters — covered with glitter and drawn with neon markers. There was no chance of missing them as you walked around the school.

Unfortunately, there was also no missing Addie, either.

She was standing in the middle of C wing handing out key chains with her picture on them. "While they were thinking about *their* website, *I* was out making presents for all of you, my fellow sixth graders," I heard her say as she handed a key chain to one girl.

She turned to a boy passing by. "I'm always thinking about you," she said, pressing a key chain into his palm and winking.

I frowned. Addie had made it seem like my friends and I were being selfish by creating a website. But that wasn't the point of the site at all. I'd made it to let everyone know how I felt about the issues. So far, Addie hadn't talked about issues at all. She'd just smiled at people and given them free stuff.

"Wow, what a great idea," I heard Celina coo as Addie handed her a key chain. "Even better than homemade cookies."

That made me mad. Celina had made me think she was on my side when I gave her my cookies. Now she was on Addie's side — just because of a stupid key chain.

Addie was trying to buy the election. And from the looks of things, it was working.

"By the way," I heard Addie say to Celina, "I love your shirt. It's just the kind of thing I would wear."

I frowned. There was nothing special about what Celina was wearing. It was just a plain sky-blue T-shirt. Addie was just saying that to get Celina to like her.

"Can I count on your vote?" I heard Addie ask her.

Celina looked at the key chain, and then at Addie's smile. "Uh, sure," she said.

"That's so cool," Addie said, thanking her in a very Pop-like way. "I always knew you were one of *us*."

Celina practically glowed at that. She looked like she'd just won the lottery or something. Which I guess she had. The middle school lottery, anyway.

MIDDLE SCHOOL RULE # 8:
EVEN PEOPLE WHO HATE POPS, WANT TO *BE* POPS.

"Addie's a piece of work, isn't she?" Chloe whispered, coming up behind me. "What a big, fat liar!"

I turned and nodded. "But people believe her. They even like her."

Chloe nodded. "Don't worry. They won't for long. Everyone is about to find out what Addie Wilson is really like."

I looked at her strangely. "What are you talking about?"

Chloe looked around. "I can't tell you now," she said, tipping her head to the left, where Dana and Claire were standing, watching us. "We'll meet at your house after school today."

Okay. Now I was really curious. I was dying to know what Chloe knew that I didn't. But I understood why she couldn't tell me anything now. There were spies every-where.

I was one of the last people to get to fifth period lunch. I'd been in the library, checking on our website. According to the counter at the bottom of our screen, 47 people had logged on so far. That wasn't bad, considering it was only 12:30, and not all the sixth graders had had their study halls yet. Study hall was about the only time you could go to the library and use the computers.

As I brought my tray over to our usual lunch table, Chloe started humming "Hail to the Chief" – the song they play whenever the real president walks into a room.

"Very funny," I said, squeezing in between her and Carolyn.

"Better get used to it," Chloe said. "You'll be president before you know it."

"If I win, it'll be because of the video on the website," I said, turning to Marc. "You're an amazing filmmaker. I look like a real candidate."

"You *are* a real candidate," Liza told me.

"You know what I mean," I said, blushing at her com-pliment. "Like in a real election. Not a school one."

"I didn't do anything. You're the one who made the video look so professional," Marc assured me. "The first thing we learned in movie club was the camera doesn't lie."

"Thanks," I said, blushing deeper. "It was really nice of you to take time out of making your movie to help me."

"Oh, I'm still making the movie," Marc explained. "The election's going to be a featured part of it. I'm going to film you making your acceptance speech when you win the election, too."

"Don't be so sure," I told him. "I've seen lots of kids carrying Addie's key chains today."

"I told you not to worry about that," Chloe insisted. She looked across the table at Marc and smiled mysteriously.

"Where's Josh?" Marilyn asked me.

"He did an awesome job on the site," Carolyn added. "I want to congratulate him."

"I think he had a Mathletes thing in the library," Marc said.

"Just as well. We need to talk about Jenny's campaign. And we don't want him knowing any of our secrets," Chloe remarked.

"We don't have any secrets," I reminded her. "All we have is a website and a cookie recipe."

"For now," Chloe said. "But there are a few more secrets coming," she added, grinning mysteriously in Marc's direction.

"I guess we can't tell Josh about them," Marc remarked with a frown.

Chloe shook her head. "Absolutely not," she declared. "He knows too much already."

I didn't see Josh all day. In fact, the first time I noticed him was in the parking lot after school. Like everyone else, he was heading toward the buses to go home. Nothing strange there – except for the fact that he was walking with Dana.

"I'm so glad you could change your plans to come to my house this time, Josh," I heard Dana say.

Josh going to Dana's house? How weird was that?

I'm pretty sure Josh knew I was staring at him as he boarded the bus, but he didn't wave or anything. He pretended he didn't see me.

But people saw him. Lots of people.

"I don't believe it," Liza said. She was standing a few feet behind me with the twins.

"Whoa," Carolyn murmured.

"Exactly what I was thinking," Marilyn told her.

"Poor Felicia," I added. I looked around quickly, to see if Felicia had seen Josh and Dana getting on the bus together. But Felicia wasn't around. She was probably still at her locker.

Phew. That was lucky.

I walked over to my bus, and grabbed seats for Felicia and me. I made sure to sit by the window so I could block her view of Dana's bus. A few moments later, Felicia climbed onto our bus and plopped down beside me.

"I was so glad I read that English chapter last night," she told me excitedly. "I've never had a surprise quiz before. They don't do that in elementary school. Half the kids in my class were totally freaked when Ms. Jaffe handed out the papers. They hadn't read anything."

I sat there listening to Felicia chatter on and on about how well she'd done on her English test. I tried to smile and act normal, but it was really hard. I knew that Chloe and Marc were coming over later to talk to me about this big campaign secret they were working on. And even though I would ordinarily ask Felicia to come to my house and hang out with us, I didn't today. If Josh really was a Pop in disguise, I couldn't risk Felicia spilling any secrets to him.

I turned slightly in my seat and caught a glimpse of Addie. She was sitting toward the back of the bus, talking to two other sixth graders. That was unusual, because Addie always sat by herself on the bus. After all, she was the only Pop on our bus, and no Pop would ever be caught dead sitting with a non-Pop. But there she was, sitting with David and Trey. That was bizarre because I knew Addie didn't like either of them. In third grade, Trey had this weird thing about picking his nose and flicking his boogers across the room. David, his best friend, always cheered him on.

Addie thought it was disgusting. And even though Trey stopped flinging boogers by fourth grade, she never really got over it.

Until now, apparently. Because there was Addie, sitting with Trey and David, happily talking about being in middle school, and how much she could do for kids like them . . . if they voted for her for sixth grade president.

"Well, I guess we could start a *Star Wars* club, if there

were enough kids who wanted it," I overheard Addie tell Trey.

"Yeah, we could get all the members Wookiee costumes," David said excitedly. "They could wear them to meetings, the way the kids on the basketball team wear their uniforms."

"Um . . . er . . . maybe," Addie replied. "Sure. Why not? Good idea, Dave."

I frowned. *Come on!* She knew the school wouldn't buy Wookiee costumes for a club. The uniforms for sports teams were totally different. But Addie would say anything at this point to get votes. And Trey and David were eating it up. They were so excited to be sitting with a Pop, they'd believe anything.

Okay, so now Addie was spending time with the kids she used to call the "gruesome twosome," just so she could convince them to vote for her. And I was sitting with Felicia, who I couldn't invite over to my house because the boy she liked might be a spy.

I'm telling you. You can't make this stuff up. Elections are weird, weird things.

Chapter SEVEN

"OKAY, SO WHAT'S THE BIG SECRET?"

It was already five o'clock, and I was busting at the seams to find out what Marc and Chloe had been hinting at during lunch.

Chloe got up from the living room couch and started walking around the room. She peered in between the flowers on the table, ran her hand over our mantel, and then bent down to look underneath the easy chair.

"What are you doing?" I asked her.

"Looking for bugs," Chloe replied.

"Bugs?" I asked, sounding very insulted. "We don't have bugs in our house, Chloe. We're very clean."

"Not those kinds of bugs," Chloe told me. "I meant recording devices. You know, like those tiny tape-recorder things you see in the movies."

"Are you crazy?" I asked. "Why would we have things like that in our living room?"

"Maybe Josh planted them in here," Chloe said. She was completely serious. "He's a real whiz when it comes to technology."

"Oh, cut it out," I said. I looked at Marc. "You don't believe Josh would do something like that, do you?"

Marc shook his head. "Come on, Chloe. You're going all drama queen on us."

"We can't be too careful," Chloe said. "You guys saw what happened today at lunch." She lifted up the cushions on the couch, looked around, and then proclaimed, "Okay, it's all clear. We can talk."

Marc looked at me and rolled his eyes. Then he took out his video camera. "I want to show you something," he said.

"Oh, you are gonna love this," Chloe said. "It's priceless."

"Show me!" I said excitedly.

Marc turned on the camera. In a second, Addie came on the small screen. She was dressed in shorts and a T-shirt, and she was dancing around her backyard with a garden hose.

"Oh, oh, oh, I'm singing in the sun. Just singing in the sun. Gonna laugh and play 'cause I'm number one," she sang out, using the end of the hose as a microphone. Then, suddenly, water splashed out of the hose, drenching her.

"See, I told you it was amazing," Chloe said.

"I don't get it," I said. "What's so special about a video of Addie singing and getting splashed?"

"It's just so totally un-Pop," Chloe said. "Especially because she sings so badly."

"Where'd you get this?" I asked Marc.

"I taped it while I was walking home from your house the other day," he said. "She never even noticed me. She never notices me. I'm not a Pop, so to her, I'm pretty much invisible."

"Which definitely works to our advantage," Chloe added. "Check out what Marc taped in school yesterday."

I watched as the video switched to the B wing hallway. Addie was talking to Claire. "Dana's not nearly as cool as she thinks she is," Addie was saying. "Like those goofy posters she made. *Addie's Rad-die.* I almost wanted to die."

Ouch. That was mean. Good thing Dana didn't hear her.

"And that's not all," Marc said proudly, as the video continued. This time, Addie was talking to Dana in C wing. "I loved all those posters you made," she was saying to Dana. "I'm so glad I picked you instead of Claire to be my campaign manager. I mean, Claire's not nearly as cool as we are. Sometimes when it rains and her hair frizzes up, she looks like a clown."

"I know," Dana said. "Her makeup is pretty circus-like, too."

"Yeah, being around her could really hurt our status," Addie agreed.

"Maybe we should keep away from her until after the election," Dana suggested.

"I think so," Addie told her. "I mean, we don't want to be seen with someone so ordinary. After all, people expect more out of me. They look up to me."

"They worship you," Dana told her.

"And you, too," Addie agreed with a giggle.

As Dana and Addie began to walk down the hall, it was hard to make out what they were saying.

"They moved out of range," Marc told me apologetically. "I didn't want to risk getting caught by following them."

"It's okay," Chloe assured him. "We got what we need, anyway."

I looked at them both strangely. "What do you mean?" I asked. "All you have is a tape of Addie and some Pops saying mean stuff. That's not exactly news."

"But they're saying mean stuff about each other," Marc said.

"Exactly," Chloe agreed. "Usually it's us they're trashing. But this time they're tearing one another apart."

"If we put this stuff on your website, everyone will see what the Pops are like when no one's watching," Marc explained. "Better yet, they'll hear themselves talking about each other."

"Divide and conquer," Chloe said. "That's their strategy with Josh. We can use the same strategy with these tapes. One look at these, and Addie's campaign is history. Even the Pops won't vote for her," Chloe declared triumphantly.

"I don't think the rest of the school will enjoy hearing that Addie thinks they worship her, either," Marc added.

"As if," Chloe seconded. "Nobody worships her."

But that wasn't true. Lots of people *did* worship Addie.

Still, Marc was right. They probably wouldn't want it thrown in their faces.

"Won't we get in trouble for taping Addie's conversations?" I asked Marc.

He shook his head. "The halls are a public space. I was just taping. Can I help it if she came into camera range?"

I knew that wasn't exactly true. He'd been looking for Addie.

"So how do you think we should get the news about this to everyone?" Chloe asked. "How about we e-mail everyone in the sixth grade and send them a link to your website?"

"Yeah, and we could tell them we have exclusive video they can only see there," Marc added excitedly.

"Exclusive. I like that," Chloe told him.

"Addie's history in this campaign," Marc assured me.

"Not only that, but the Pops will be furious with her," Chloe continued. "They'll ditch her. She'll be totally friendless."

I studied Chloe's face. I don't think I'd ever seen her this happy. Which was kind of weird because the thing that was making her so happy was being mean to someone else. This had gone way beyond a campaign for class president.

I frowned slightly. "Maybe we should wait and think about this."

"There's no time to waste," Chloe told me. "The

election's next week. We want people to see this tape right away."

I didn't say anything.

"Don't we?" Chloe asked me.

"I'm not sure," I said honestly. "It will hurt a lot of people's feelings to see this. And it was kind of sneaky to tape Addie when she didn't know she was being filmed."

"I was standing right there, with my camera. I can't help it if she didn't notice me," Marc defended himself.

"I know, but . . ."

"Jenny, do you want to win this election or not?" Chloe demanded.

"Of course I do."

"Then this tape is really important. Because right now, people are liking Addie . . . *a lot.*"

"That's because she's giving them key chains and telling them whatever they want to hear," I insisted. "She's not talking about any real issues."

"Apparently people don't want to hear about school dances or field days," Chloe told me. "They're voting for Addie because she's a Pop."

"And no matter how many great ideas you have, that's one thing you'll never be," Marc added.

"Neither will you!" I muttered.

"But I'm not running for class president," Marc said.

"I don't get your attitude, Jenny," Chloe told me. "This is what we've been waiting for!"

I took a deep breath. "Just let me think about it,

okay?" I asked them. "I promise I'll decide what to do by tomorrow."

Chloe and Marc didn't stay at my house much longer after that. Before I knew it, I was all alone in the living room.

I had a big decision to make. And I had no clue what the right answer was. So, I did what I'd been doing lately. I went on the computer.

What was it Chloe had said? Something about how she didn't get my attitude about all this. Well, I didn't, either. Mostly because I didn't know what my attitude about all this was.

Luckily, there was a middleschoolsurvival.com quiz that could help me figure it all out.

Dude, Do You Have A Major 'Tude?

Answer these questions to find out what kind of attitude you have.

1. You love softball and want to join the girls' team. But no one goes to girls' games at your school. What do you do?

    A. Forget about playing and join the gang in the stands at the boys' baseball games.

    B. Try to get your friends to support the girls' team and come out to cheer.

    C. You don't need anyone's approval. Go out, join the team, and pitch that no-hitter.

I figured my answer had to be B. I'm not a great athlete, but I do think girls' teams should get attention, too.

2. You've just walked out of the local grocery store with a cold soda in your hand. You see an older person struggling with her packages. Do you

    A. Let the clerk in the store know so he can send someone to help.

B. Keep on going. Much as you'd like to help, you've got plans and you can't be late.
C. Put down your can of soda and give the woman a hand. How long can it take?

I would be the kind of person who would help the old woman. At least I hoped that's what I would do. I clicked C. I was pretty sure that was how I'd handle things.

3. Okay, so you were really tired this morning and accidentally put on a purple sweater and orange socks. The fashion police at school are sure to give you a hard time. Do you

A. Keep a low profile for the day.
B. Not care at all. You're your own person. You can wear whatever you choose with complete confidence.
C. Make a joke out of your look and beat the critics to the punch.

A few weeks ago I would have clicked A, because Addie and her friends had a way of making me feel really lousy about myself. But lately I'd learned to pretty much ignore them. I clicked C. I might not feel good about my fashion faux pas, but I could definitely laugh about it.

4. You hear on the evening news about a horrible tornado that has destroyed a town somewhere on the other side of the country. What's your reaction?

A. Write down the address of where your parents can send a donation.
B. Organize a relief effort at school.
C. Immediately find the remote. This is too depressing to watch.

Last year a big earthquake had destroyed a town in Asia. My whole class got together and had a bake sale and a car wash to raise money to help the people there. I was very involved in that. So my answer was a definite B.

5. There's a new girl in school who is incredibly shy. What's your game plan?

A. Ignore her completely. You've got plenty of friends already.
B. Smile at her in gym class, just to let her know you're an approachable person.
C. Invite her to sit at a table with you and your friends for lunch.

I remembered how great it felt when Chloe came up and asked me to sit with her friends at the beginning of school. Before then I'd eaten alone – in the stairwell, at the library, and even sitting in a phone booth. Eating alone at school really stinks. C, I would invite the new girl to sit with us for sure.

I clicked on the SUBMIT button and waited for the computer to tally up my points.

Check out how many points each of your answers is worth. Then add up your score, and check where you land on the 'tude meter.

Here are the point values for each answer.

1. A) 1 B) 2 C) 3
2. A) 2 B) 1 C) 3
3. A) 1 B) 3 C) 2
4. A) 2 B) 3 C) 1
5. A) 1 B) 2 C) 3

12–15 points: Congratulations! You are the queen of self-esteem. And better yet, your positive 'tude allows you the confidence to help others, even when it may not be the popular thing to do. You'd never go out of your way to hurt someone else. You don't need to do that just to build yourself up. You're already confident.

8–11 points: You're a fascinating mix. At times, you can be incredibly kind and giving, with a generous attitude that people adore. At other times, a lack of motivation keeps you thinking of yourself. Basically, you're human — not perfect, but well on your way to being the kind of gal who's not so stuck on herself that she can't take the time to help others.

5-7 points: Time for an attitude adustment. You're far too wrapped up in yourself. Open your eyes and notice the world around you. You just might like what you see.

I had scored 13 points. Wow! I had no idea I was that confident. But the part that really stuck with me was that thing about not going out of my way to hurt somebody else. That's definitely what I would be doing if I let Marc and Chloe put that video on my website. And as much as I wanted to win, I just couldn't do it that way. Fighting dirty like that was the kind of thing Addie and her friends might do. I wasn't going to sink that low. No way.

I had made my decision. I just hoped I wasn't going to be sorry about it later.

Chloe could barely even look at me as she, Felicia, Rachel, and I walked into school together on Friday morning. Instead, Chloe was laughing at Rachel's jokes, which was definitely weird, because Chloe usually thought Rachel's jokes were pretty bad.

"So what did the sock say to the foot?" Rachel asked us.

"What?" Felicia wondered.

"You're putting me on."

Felicia and I looked at each other and sighed. Another bad joke from Rachel . . . but you had to love her.

But Chloe laughed as if it were the funniest thing she'd ever heard.

If Felicia and Rachel sensed any tension between Chloe and me, they didn't show it. To break the ice, I turned to Chloe and said, "We gotta get to English. We're going to be late."

"Whatever," Chloe replied, rolling her eyes. She turned

to Felicia and Rachel. "See you later," she added. Then she stomped down the hall, leaving me three steps behind her.

Boy, Chloe really was furious about my decision not to use the tape of Addie. Which was kinda funny, because Marc wasn't angry at all. And he was the one who'd taken the video in the first place. He'd just shrugged and said he'd still help me in any way he could.

But as far as Chloe was concerned, this had turned into more than just a campaign. This was a mission. She wanted to be the one to take down the Pops. And she was mad that I'd taken away the "secret weapon."

I had always thought Chloe didn't care what the Pops said or thought about her. Obviously, I was wrong. Nobody got this mad without caring.

"So, anyway, I was thinking we could have a big party to celebrate after you win," Dana said loudly, as Chloe and I entered English class. I could tell she wanted to make sure everyone heard her conversation. "Maybe a pool party at Claire's house. It'll still be warm by next week, don't you think?"

"Mmm-hmm. We would just invite the people who voted for us, right?" Addie added in an equally loud voice.

I could see the eyes of the kids in our sixth grade English class light up. The idea of being invited to a Pops party was something that they'd barely even dared to dream about.

"I guess that doesn't include those two," Dana said, pointing to Chloe and me.

"No losers at the luau," Addie added.

"You see what we're up against?" Chloe hissed angrily in my ear. "Everyone's going to want to go to that party."

I nodded. I understood. But I also didn't want to sink that low. I wanted to be elected president because I was the right person for the job — not because I'd destroyed Addie Wilson.

Not that it hadn't been tempting.

Chapter
{EIGHT}

"HEY, MARILYN, MOVE OVER, WOULD YOU?" Josh asked, as he walked over to our lunch table that afternoon.

Marilyn glanced at Chloe. Chloe shrugged and stared at her sandwich with intense fascination. It was like there was nothing more amazing than tuna on whole wheat. Marilyn didn't know what to do.

Josh just stood there for a minute watching everyone. Finally, Liza scooted over to make room for him. "Here you go," she said in her quiet, peaceful voice.

Usually, we're a pretty rowdy group at lunch. But today no one was talking. Chloe was too mad at me and too paranoid about Josh to say anything. Marilyn and Carolyn were pretty much convinced Josh was a spy, too, and so they kept their distance. Marc was busy reading his English book, getting ready for his test next period.

Only Liza seemed completely normal around Josh. She was too nice to believe that one of her friends could have gone over to the dark side. "How's the Mathlete club going?" she asked.

"Pretty good. I'm the youngest one in the club, but I'm holding my own," he told her.

"I'm sure you're going to be fine," Liza assured Josh. "You pick stuff up really quickly."

Josh smiled at her and shoved a forkful of spaghetti into his mouth. We all kept eating in silence.

It was definitely uncomfortable at the table. But I was glad Josh was there. With him around, Chloe wouldn't dare mention the videotape. And that meant she wouldn't be able to bug me about my decision.

"Okay, I'm done," Marilyn said. She turned to her sister. "You ready?"

Carolyn smiled. "Oh, yeah!" She reached under the table and pulled out a big black portable CD player. "Here we go."

With a push of a button, the music began. Everyone in the cafeteria grew quiet as the song "We Are the Champions" by Queen blasted through the room. You know, it's that song they play at ball games and stuff.

Everyone looked up, surprised. Our cafeteria is usually loud, but only with the sound of kids talking. The music got everyone's attention big-time! Already a group of kids had leaped up on their chairs. They were waving their arms back and forth in the air and singing, "We are the champions. We are the champions. . . ."

Mrs. Martinez, a science teacher, ran over and made them all sit down. The kids did as they were told. But they didn't totally calm down.

"What's this?" I asked.

"It was Marilyn's idea," Liza said. "Or maybe it was Carolyn's. I can't remember. But we burned a whole bunch of CDs on their computer, and put these stickers on the cases." She handed me a CD.

"SAVE OUR SCHOOL. LET JENNY RULE!" I read from the sticker. "Wow, that's great!"

"I designed the stickers. We figured everybody loves that song. Who wouldn't want it on CD?" Liza said.

"Totally!" I agreed. "The sticker is a great touch."

"Yeah," Chloe said, sounding sincerely impressed.

"We wanted to surprise you, Jenny," Liza said.

I smiled at her. I had the best friends in the whole world.

"I wish you guys had let me know about this last night," Josh said. "I could have bought the song online and down-loaded it onto Jenny's website. We could have made it her theme song."

"Hello? Liza just said it was a *surprise*," Chloe told him angrily. "And besides, it's not like we have to tell you every-thing we're planning."

Josh looked at her oddly. "What's with her?" he asked Marc.

Marc shrugged and went back to studying.

A few moments later, Dana approached our table. She made a point of ignoring all of us — except Josh, that is.

"There you are, Joshie," she said sweetly. "I was look-ing for you."

I glanced across the table at Chloe. *Joshie?* I mouthed silently.

Chloe shrugged and rolled her eyes.

"You were looking for me? Why?" he asked her.

"To thank you for yesterday afternoon," she replied. "I can't wait to get together again today after school."

Josh looked from Dana to the rest of us. We were all just sitting there, staring.

"We were just, uh . . ." Josh began.

"Oh, they're not interested in what we were doing," Dana assured him.

"She's got that right," Chloe huffed. "We couldn't care less."

"Exactly," Dana agreed. "But, Josh, you and I still have to talk about a few problems I'm having. Do you think you can sit at our table, so we can figure it out?"

Josh looked nervously at us.

"Go ahead," Chloe said. "We're squished here, anyway."

Josh frowned slightly, then stood and picked up his tray. "Sure, no problem," he told Dana.

"Whoa," Marc muttered beneath his breath. "That's a first."

I knew what he meant. Josh was going to eat lunch at the Pops' table, with Addie, Claire, Jeffrey, Aaron, and the rest of them. I couldn't believe it.

MIDDLE SCHOOL RULE # 9:
POPS NEVER INVITE NON-POPS TO SIT WITH THEM!

I couldn't believe Josh was leaving us to go sit with them. After all, the Pops were our sworn enemies. Still, I had to wonder, if given the chance, just how many of us would do the exact same thing? Even after everything that had gone on between Addie and me, there was still a little part of me that wished I could be one of them.

But I wasn't. None of my friends were. *At least not until today, anyway.*

"I am so dreading getting on that school bus this afternoon," I said, watching Josh and Dana sit down at the Pops table. "How am I supposed to sit next to Felicia and not tell her about all this?"

"Just be glad she has a different lunch period and doesn't have to see them," Chloe said. "I'm sorry I do. Looking at them is making me lose my appetite."

"It's not your fault," Liza reminded me.

"It's not your job to tell her, either," Marc told me. "It's between her and Josh."

"Will you all stop thinking about Josh! We've got a campaign to work on," Chloe reminded us. She looked over at the dancing kids, who were eagerly snatching CDs from the twins' hands. "You owe it to our class to win this election."

"Yeah. You've got to get going on your speech," Marc reminded me. "Did you and Felicia write it yet?"

"Most of it," I told him.

A furious look came over Chloe's face. "Most of it? Most

of it?" she demanded. "First, you won't let Marc use the secret weapon on our website, and now you don't even take the time to write a whole speech? You should be done by now! The election is only a few days away!" Chloe rolled her eyes toward the sky and then buried her head in her arms on the cafeteria table. "Oh, why do I bother?"

"Ah, the drama queen strikes again," Marc groaned. "Give us a break, Chloe. Save it for the play auditions."

Chloe scowled at him and then turned her attention toward me. "Jenny, you should be glad I'm your campaign manager. Otherwise nothing would get done."

"I *am* glad all of you guys are around," I said honestly. "This election wouldn't have been any fun without you."

Chloe's eyes lit up with anger again. "I can't believe you just said that!" she exclaimed.

"What?" I asked her. "All I said was . . ."

"It's not about *fun*, Jenny," Chloe interrupted me. "It's about winning!" She began pounding her fist against the table, harder and harder and then . . .

Splat! Chloe's fist came down right on an open ketchup packet. Red, gooey ketchup spurted up into the air. It landed all over her hair and face.

Liza, Marc, and I began to laugh hysterically. Marc pulled out his video camera and began shooting footage of Chloe covered in dark red goo.

"Looks like this campaign is getting bloody, folks," he joked.

{Chapter NINE}

ON SATURDAY MORNING, Team Jenny (as Chloe had started to call us) gathered at my house. I was going to practice my speech. My friends were going to be my audience.

"Now don't forget to speak slowly," Rachel warned. "People can't understand if you speak too fast."

"And be sure you stop for laughter after your joke," Chloe said. "Give people the chance to love you."

"What if they don't laugh?" I asked her nervously.

"They'll laugh," Chloe assured me. "*I* wrote the joke."

"Oh, I wish you'd let me know you needed a joke," Rachel said. "I have lots of them."

"We know," Chloe told her. "But this one's better."

Rachel scowled, but said nothing. There was no point arguing with Chloe when she was in campaign-manager mode.

"The rest of the speech is pretty great, too," Felicia told our friends. "I wrote it — with Jenny, of course."

"I thought you were going to get Josh to help you, too," Rachel mentioned to me. "Where is he?"

Marilyn and Carolyn frowned and looked at the ground. Marc fiddled with his video camera. Chloe, Liza, and I exchanged glances. Rachel didn't have the same lunch period. So she didn't know what was going on with Josh and Dana.

Not that we really knew what was happening, either.

"He . . . um . . . he has a tae kwon do class," Chloe lied.

"No, he doesn't," Felicia corrected her. "That class is on Wednesdays."

"It's a . . . er . . . a makeup class," Carolyn suggested.

"Yeah, 'cause he missed a few sessions over the summer," Marilyn added.

"He didn't say anything about a makeup class," Felicia replied. "Of course, I hardly got to talk to Josh this week. He's been kinda busy."

"Gee, I wonder with *who*?" Chloe mumbled under her breath.

"What?" Felicia asked her.

"Let's get started on this speech," I said, changing the subject.

"You get started," Felicia said. "I'll be right back." She started walking toward the hall closet.

"Where are you going?" I asked her.

"To get my cell phone," Felicia replied.

As she walked out of the room, Marc glanced anxiously at Chloe. "She's gonna call Josh," he said.

Chloe grinned. "Don't worry. It's been taken care of."

"What's taken care of?" Rachel asked.

"Uh, nothing," Marc said.

"We'll tell you later," Chloe added. "Jenny, you should start your speech now."

"Yeah," Marc agreed, holding up his camera. "I'm gonna tape you. Then we can watch the tape and figure out what's working and what's not."

"Okay," I said, nervously standing up.

"Now I'm going to introduce you, just the way I'm going to do during the real thing," Chloe said, leaping to her feet. She stood up and looked at Marc. "You'd better tape me, too," she said. "I need to be sure I'm convincing."

Marc rolled his eyes. "No one cares how you sound," he told Chloe.

"Oh, yes they do. Jenny's introduction is very important. So . . ."

Just then, Felicia wandered back into the room. "That's so strange," she said. "I was sure I put my phone in my jacket pocket, but it's not there now."

"Maybe you just forgot it," Chloe said.

"I don't think so," Felicia said. "My mom reminded me twice to bring it."

"Just call Josh from Jenny's home phone," Rachel suggested.

"I don't know his number by heart. It's in my phone," Felicia explained. "Any of you guys have it?" she asked us.

"Not me," Marilyn said.

"Me, neither," Carolyn echoed.

"I have it written down at home," Liza told her.

"Don't worry, we'll get his number later," Marc said. "Just sit down and listen to Jenny's speech."

"Okay," Chloe said, as Felicia plopped down on the floor.

"Now, I'll stand up and walk over to the microphone. Then I'll wait a minute for all the applause to die down . . ."

"Applause?" Carolyn asked. "For you?"

"*Jenny's* the candidate, remember?" Marilyn added.

Chloe sighed but didn't respond. Instead, she started her introduction, "I'd like to introduce you to your next sixth grade president – a girl who is honest and kind. Someone who represents all of us. Someone who doesn't spend her whole lunch period putting on makeup in the bathroom. She's too busy thinking about how to help our school to worry about lip gloss and eyeliner. And that's the kind of person we want for class president. Ladies and gentlemen, I give you Jenny McAfee!"

"Yeah!"

"Jenny rocks!"

"Jenny! Jenny! Jenny!"

As my friends cheered, I stood up and started my speech.

"Thank you, Chloe," I said, turning to smile at her. "Can I get a copy of that for my parents? I'd like to give them that instead of my next report card." I waited for the laughter, like Chloe had told me to.

Unfortunately, Chloe was the only one who laughed.

"*That's* your big joke?" Marc asked Chloe.

"It's funny," Chloe insisted. "You guys just don't have a sense of humor."

"That's not the problem," Marc replied.

"Jenny, go on," Liza said, before Marc and Chloe could get into it again.

"I am running for sixth grade class president because I believe that we can make this the best school in the world," I said, reading from my speech. "And as the youngest kids in this school, we have the most to gain from making some positive changes right now. After all, we'll be the ones who can benefit from them for three whole . . ."

Just then I heard faint music playing. Weird. The music seemed to be coming from the flowerpot on the windowsill.

"That's my ring tone," Felicia said, leaping up from the couch and walking over to the window. She peeked into the flowerpot. "How'd my phone get in there?" she asked.

I caught a glimpse of Chloe biting her lip and kicking at the floor. So that was what she'd meant when she said it had been taken care of.

"Well, at least I've got it back now," Felicia said. "But I can't imagine how it got there."

"Maybe it fell out of your jacket pocket into the flowerpot," Chloe suggested.

"My jacket was in the other room," Felicia said. She eyed Chloe suspiciously. "You didn't take my phone, did you?"

"What do you need a phone so badly for, anyway?" Chloe asked, deliberately not answering her question.

"So I can call Josh and tell him to come over," Felicia explained.

"No!" Chloe shouted.

"Huh?" Felicia was confused.

"She . . . er . . . she just meant that we can't wait for him. Jenny's already started her speech," Liza told her.

"So? He can come over and watch the tape with us later," Felicia reasoned. "He'll have some good suggestions."

"We don't want Josh here, okay?" Chloe said finally.

"Chloe . . ." I started.

"Look, enough's enough," Chloe said. "She may as well know."

"I may as well know what?" Felicia asked.

"That Josh is definitely a spy for Addie's side," Chloe told her.

"Oh, that again," Felicia said. "Jenny and I already talked about that. And it's not true. We took a test on the computer to prove that he still likes me. Which means he can't be a spy."

"Yeah, well, did the computer tell you he ate lunch at the Pops' table yesterday and hung out with Dana after school?" Chloe continued.

Felicia looked like she was going to cry. She looked at Rachel and me. "Did you guys know this?"

"This is news to me," Rachel said.

I frowned. "She did ask him to eat at the Pops' table, but we don't really know . . ."

Marilyn smiled at Felicia. "Look, maybe it's nothing, you know?"

"But just to be safe, maybe we shouldn't let Josh hear Jenny's speech, okay?" Carolyn said, finishing her sister's thought.

Felicia frowned. "Whatever." She turned and headed toward the door.

"Where are you going?" I asked her.

"Home. I don't want to hear the speech, either."

"Come on, Felicia, stay," Marc said. "Just 'cause you're mad at Josh doesn't . . ."

"I'm *more* mad at you guys," Felicia said.

"Us?" I asked her. "Why?"

"Because none of you told me about Josh and Dana having lunch together," Felicia said. "So maybe you don't trust me, either."

"That's not it," I said. "I just didn't want you to feel bad. Your feelings were so hurt the first time we mentioned that he might be a spy, remember?"

"Well, my feelings are definitely hurt. But this time I feel bad about Josh, *and* about you keeping secrets from me," Felicia shouted. "So I guess you're not telling me only made things worse."

Talk about an understatement.

"I'm going home!" she shouted, as she stormed out of my house.

"Such a drama queen," Chloe groaned.

Marc rolled his eyes. "Takes one to know one."

"What's that supposed to mean?" Chloe countered.

I looked at both of them and shook my head. "I'm sick of all this fighting," I said. Then I headed toward the door.

"Now where are *you* going?" Chloe asked.

"To talk to Felicia," I replied.

"You can't. We have to work on this speech," Chloe told me. "We haven't even gotten through it once yet. And you have to make the speech on Monday."

I gulped. Monday was just two days away.

Chloe was right. Besides, Felicia was too mad to listen to me right now, anyway. So I read the speech over and over and over, until my mouth was dry and my tongue was tired. Then we watched the tape, talked about what changes I could make, and I read the speech again.

By the time everyone went home, I was exhausted. And I couldn't wait for the whole election to be over.

My telephone rang first thing Sunday morning — before I was even out of bed. I leaped up to answer it before the call woke my parents.

I was hoping it was Felicia calling to say she wasn't mad anymore. I'm not very good at being in fights.

"Hey, are you awake yet?" the person on the other end of the phone said.

"I am now," I said groggily. I sighed slightly. It was Chloe.

"I was thinking about your speech," Chloe said. "It's good, but it might not be good enough."

"I'm not changing my speech now," I told her. "I had enough trouble writing this one."

"I know there's no time to change the speech. And it's great – really," Chloe assured me. "I just don't know if it's good enough to win this election. People are really into being invited to a Pops party. They'll vote for Addie just for that."

"Well, we can say we'll have a victory party, too," I said.

"It's not the same thing," Chloe said. "Jen, I really wish you would reconsider using Marc's tape. We'd be doing the public a favor by showing them the real Addie Wilson."

I frowned. Chloe was right. Addie was a creep. But she hadn't always been. It made me sad to think about how my former best friend was acting these days.

"Yeah, but if I use that tape, I'll be just as bad," I told Chloe.

"Not as far as I'm concerned," Chloe assured me. "I figure all's fair in politics. If Addie had a tape like this, don't you think she'd use it?"

I didn't know the answer to that one. After all, Addie and I might be running against each other for sixth grade president, and we might not like each other anymore, but I think Addie still had some good memories of when we'd been friends. I know I did.

I had to hope those memories would keep Addie from being as mean as Chloe thought she could be.

{ Chapter TEN }

THE PICTURES WERE the first thing I saw when I walked into school Monday morning. They were everywhere — huge, giant color photos of me.

But these weren't pictures my friends posted on the walls. These were put up by the Pops. No one else would be so cruel.

There was a huge one of me at age nine with underpants on my head. My pigtails were sticking out of the holes where your legs go.

I knew exactly when that picture was taken. It was at a sleepover at Addie's house. Addie was originally in the picture with underpants on her head, too. But she'd cut herself out of the shot before blowing it up poster-size.

And that wasn't even the worst picture. Farther down the hall, there was a photo of me with my hair standing straight up in the air. I looked like some sort of monster.

Of course, what you couldn't see was Addie standing over me with a balloon in her hand. That picture was taken the day we'd been doing our static-electricity project for fifth grade science. There was a picture of Addie with her hair standing on end, too. But that one wasn't on the wall.

The last picture was of me with my cheeks all blown up like a chipmunk and a tiny bubble-gum bubble coming out of my mouth. My face was bright red and my eyes were bulging out of my head.

Addie's mom had taken that one. It was the day Mr. Wilson had taught Addie and me how to blow bubbles with gum. The picture of Addie had been even worse, because her eyes were crossed. But I didn't see that photo anywhere.

The last poster on the wall didn't have any pictures on it at all. Instead it read:

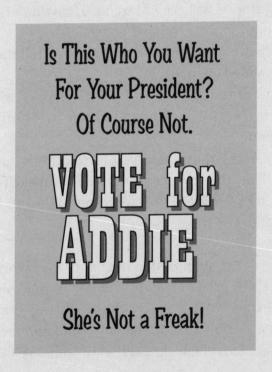

Is This Who You Want
For Your President?
Of Course Not.

VOTE for ADDIE

She's Not a Freak!

Now I was mad. Really mad. It wasn't the pictures so much — although they were really awful. It was more that Addie had used pictures of us when we were friends to make fun of me. Like the whole eight years that we were best friends was some kind of joke! I don't think I'd ever been angrier at anyone in my whole life.

Addie Wilson was a real jerk. A supercolossal jerk. A humongous mega-jerk!

"Still wanna forget about using that video?" Chloe asked me, as she walked over and stood by my side.

"I've got it right here," Marc said, patting his camera. "We can put it online right after school."

"And then call all the sixth graders and tell them about it," Chloe added excitedly.

I looked at the posters lining the walls of C wing. I had a feeling there were more just like them in the other wings of the school.

"Don't erase that video yet," I told Marc and Chloe. "Let's see how the speeches go. If Addie's speech is half as mean as these posters are, we're not going to have any choice but to use it."

"Okay, so I'm supposed to introduce my favorite candidate for sixth grade class president," Dana said, as she stood in front of the microphone during the election speeches assembly that afternoon. "But I don't really have to do that. Everybody knows who Addie Wilson is! So all I'm going to say is – here's your next sixth grade president!"

As the kids applauded, Addie stood up and waved her hand like she was some sort of queen greeting her royal subjects. Then she flashed her big, white toothy smile and began her speech.

"I guess everyone knows by now that I'm running for sixth grade president," she said. "I could stand up here and make a whole bunch of campaign promises that I'll never be able to keep, which is probably what my opponent is going to do. But that would be long, boring, and a complete waste of time. I want to keep my speech nice and short."

The kids in the audience applauded loudly at that.

Addie laughed. "Anyway, let me just tell you why I'm the perfect person to represent the sixth grade in student government. It's all about my image. We want the seventh and eighth graders to think our class is really cool. And I know you'll all agree that, of the two candidates running for this office, I'm the cool one."

I frowned slightly. I couldn't argue with Addie's logic. She sure did look cool and calm up there while she made her speech. *I* certainly wasn't calm. I was a nervous wreck. What if I burped in the middle of talking? What if I got the hiccups and couldn't stop. What if I threw up? I was feeling kinda nauseous.

"Anyhow, to sum it up, we sixth graders don't want to

be thought of as babies by the rest of the school. And since I'm really mature, I'd be the best person to represent you – the sixth grade class – in our student government. Thank you."

The kids started to clap then. Addie smiled and took a deep bow. As she turned around, she shot me a victorious look. I turned away and tried not to think about how jumpy my stomach was.

Chloe stepped up to the mike and made her introductory speech. Then, after she'd said all those nice things about me, I stood up and walked toward the front of the stage.

"Don't forget to wait for the laughter after the joke," Chloe whispered to me as she went to sit down in her seat.

I nodded, but I knew I wasn't going to have to wait for laughter. After seeing those mean, horrible posters in the hall, I'd made a few changes in my speech. And I hadn't told anyone – not even my campaign manager, Chloe – about it.

I waited for a minute, took a deep breath, and then began to read from my note cards.

"Appealing to or appreciated by a wide range of people. Relating to the general public," I read slowly off my note card. Then I looked up at the audience. "That's the definition of the word 'popular' – at least according to the dictionary. Addie Wilson may think she's the most popular girl in the sixth grade, or maybe even in the whole school, but being popular isn't about who has the best eyeliner, or who wears the most expensive clothes. It's about being able to relate to a lot of people. And according to that definition, I'm a whole lot more popular than Addie Wilson."

I could feel Addie tensing up in her chair as she sat behind me. I knew she never thought I'd have the guts to fight her over who was more popular. But I did. And I had a whole lot more to say about it, too.

" I – like most of you – care about a lot more than just makeup and clothes. And I don't think it's fun to hang out in the bathroom during lunch talking about people. But I do like having a good time – even if it means getting a little goofy or silly." I paused for a minute, just for effect. "And that includes putting underwear on my head and dancing around the room when I'm at a sleepover."

I turned around and looked at Addie. "Remember when we *both* did that, Addie? In fact, I think that's your underwear on my head in the picture that's hanging in C wing."

The kids all laughed. Addie blushed and looked down at the ground.

I smiled and turned back to the audience. "Just like you guys, I care about Joyce Kilmer Middle School. I want to make it a great place to be. And I've got a few ideas about just how we can do that."

The rest of my speech was just the way I'd rehearsed it over the weekend. I gave my thoughts on student lounges, and a fairer method for sign-ups for clubs. I talked about getting a healthier menu in the cafeteria, and annual field days for each grade. And when I was finished, everyone in the audience was clapping. A lot of people even stood up to cheer for me.

Whoa! A standing ovation. I never thought that would happen!

I took a deep breath. I'd done it! I'd made my speech without burping or throwing up. I'd been able to make fun of myself, which took the sting out of the mean posters Addie and her friends had put up on the walls. Most of all, I'd been able to let everyone know my great ideas for how to make our school better.

I didn't know who was going to win this election, but I was certain I had done the right thing.

MIDDLE SCHOOL RULE # 10:
WHEN IN DOUBT, BE YOURSELF.
THAT WAY YOU CAN'T LOSE!

"Great speech, Jenny!" Josh was the first person to congratulate me as I walked off the stage with Chloe.

"Thanks," I replied.

"Bet you're disappointed you didn't know what she was going to say ahead of time," Chloe barked at him.

"Huh? Why?" Josh asked her.

"So you could tell your *girlfriend* about Jenny's ideas for the school," Chloe said.

"My girlfriend?" Josh sounded genuinely confused.

"Yeah, you know, *Dana*," Chloe said.

"Dana?" Josh asked.

"Yes, *Joshie*," Chloe continued. "We know she's been using you to spy on Jenny's campaign. But Jenny kept this speech a secret – even from me. And now Addie doesn't stand a chance."

"I hate Dana and Addie," Josh insisted.

"Oh, yeah?" Chloe demanded. "Then why have you been eating lunch with Dana and seeing her after school?"

Josh took a deep breath, then answered, "Because I'm her math tutor."

"Her *what*?" Chloe asked. Now it was her turn to sound confused.

"Her math tutor," Josh repeated. "She was failing math, so I was teaching her after school. Everyone in the Mathletes has to tutor somebody. It's part of being in the club."

"But why Dana? Why didn't you tell us?" I asked him.

Josh shrugged. "I didn't have a choice. Dana was the one I got assigned to. And I knew it would upset you guys, so I tried to hide it."

"If you were *only* her tutor, how come Dana was acting all mushy around you – giving you candy and asking you to eat lunch with her?" Chloe demanded, not believing Josh's story.

"I don't know. Maybe she wanted you to think I was on her side," Josh suggested. "To make you mad at me or something."

I frowned. If that's what Addie and Dana had in mind, it sure had worked.

"Or maybe she was just grateful that I helped her pass her math test. But she's not my girlfriend, and I'm no spy!" Josh was practically shouting now.

I could feel the red rushing up in my cheeks. I was really ashamed. I couldn't believe I'd actually thought such awful things about Josh.

Worse yet, now Felicia believed it, too. *What a mess.* We'd all let this election get in the way of our friendships.

Well, that was going to stop right now!

"Josh, I'm so sorry," I told him sincerely. Then I turned and headed toward the back of the auditorium, where Felicia and Rachel were standing.

"Where are you going?" Chloe asked me.

"I have to talk to someone," I told her.

"But I thought you were going to stay and shake hands with people," Chloe said. "We don't have much time before tomorrow's election."

"I will," I assured her. "But right now, I have something much more important to do."

Chapter ELEVEN

I BARELY GOT ANY SLEEP Monday night. Every time I closed my eyes, I had weird dreams. In some of them, Addie won the election, and she tortured me about it by making me run around school with giant granny panties on my head.

In some of the dreams I won, and then I actually had to be the president – which was something I didn't have a clue about how to do. I kept running around and around the school in circles, looking for the student government office and never finding it.

Either way, I was running and I didn't know where I was going. I hate dreams like that.

When my alarm clock finally rang at 7:00 Tuesday morning, I sat up in bed like a shot. Election day was here. There was nothing more I could do or say to change things. It was all up to the voters now.

It was kind of funny. I'd gotten into the race just to beat Addie and the Pops. But now that it was all over, I wanted to win because I really wanted to make Joyce Kilmer a better place to go to school. At least for most of us. The Pops already thought it was a great place. They were the ones who ruled the school.

At least they did until now . . . *I hoped.*

But I wasn't going to find out for sure who'd won until the end of the school day. That was when all the votes would be tallied, and the winner would be announced over the loudspeaker. But there were a whole lot of hours between now and then. How was I ever going to make it until the end of school?

"Are you ready to vote?" Chloe greeted Felicia and I as we walked from our bus to the school building later that morning.

I nodded. "Did you vote already?"

Chloe shook her head. "Uh-uh. I was waiting for you guys to get here. But we'd better hurry. The line in the cafeteria is getting really long."

As we turned toward the building, we saw Addie, Dana, and Claire walking just ahead of us to the school.

"Oh, get a load of her," Chloe added, pointing toward Addie. "What does she think this is? The Academy Awards?"

I had to laugh. Addie was dressed as though she were about to walk the red carpet. Her long blond hair hung down her back in a neat French braid. And instead of her usual jeans and shirt, she was wearing a really pretty dress.

I looked down at my jeans, T-shirt, and red sneakers. "I didn't know we were supposed to dress up for this," I said.

"You look exactly the way you're supposed to. You're one of the people, remember?" Felicia assured me.

"Okay, let's get this all on video," Marc said as he and Josh came up beside us. "The candidate casts a vote for herself," he announced into the camera microphone.

"How do you know who I'm voting for?" I asked him. "It's a secret ballot. Maybe I think Addie's the right . . ."

"What?!" Chloe exclaimed. "Of course you're going to vote for yourself. You have to! What if you lost by one vote? Then you'd feel awful and —"

"Relax, Chloe." I laughed. "I was just joking."

"Don't kid around about stuff like that," Chloe said, catching her breath. "It's not funny."

I walked over to the table in the cafeteria where the ballots were stacked up. Two teachers were sitting there, making sure each sixth grader only voted once. I stood there for a moment, looking at the ballot. There were only two names on it. Addie Wilson and Jenny McAffee. Quickly, I checked the box next to my name, dropped it in the box, and walked away.

That was it. All the speechwriting, cookie-baking, tape-making, and handshaking was finished. There was nothing left for me to do but wait.

That was going to be the hardest part.

Later that afternoon, our Spanish class was interrupted by a messenger from the principal's office.

"Jenny, will you go to Principal Gold's office, *por favor*?" Señorita Gonzalez said after reading the note.

"Oooo . . ." A bunch of boys in the back of the room

teased as I collected my books and headed for the door. "Jenny's in trouble!"

"*Clase*," Señorita Gonzalez warned. "*Silencio*."

Chloe shot me a questioning look as I passed by her desk. I shrugged. I really had no idea what this was all about. I knew I hadn't done anything wrong. So why was I being called to the principal's office?

It had to be about the election. As I walked down the hall, my mind began to race. Did I win by a landslide? Or had I lost so badly that Principal Gold wanted to personally let me down easy?

When I got to Principal Gold's office, Addie was already in the waiting room. I could tell by the expression on her face that she was just as nervous and confused.

"If we're both here, it must have something to do with the election," I said.

"She's probably going to let you have it," Addie said smugly.

"Me?" I asked her. "What did I do?

"You and your friends drew all over *my* posters," Addie said. "Remember?"

"I told you that wasn't us," I reminded her. "Besides, maybe she's gonna yell at *you* for putting up those awful pictures of me all over the school."

"Those weren't mean," Addie said — a little too sweetly. "I thought they were cute."

"Yeah, right," I huffed. "If they were so cute, why'd you cut yourself out of them?"

Before Addie could answer me, Principal Gold opened the door to her office. "Oh, good, you're both here. Won't you come in, girls?"

I took a deep breath and stood up. This wasn't the first time I'd been in Principal Gold's office. The last time I was here, it was because Addie and I had gotten into a food fight in the cafeteria. Principal Gold had been plenty mad at us that time. Ugh. I could feel my stomach tensing up just thinking about that day.

"Take a seat, please," the principal said, pointing to two wooden chairs on the other side of her desk. "There's something we need to talk about."

Addie and I didn't even look at each other as we sat down. We both just kept staring at Principal Gold, wondering what this was all about.

"I have the results of this year's sixth grade presidential election," the principal told us. "And I wanted to talk to both of you before I announced them."

Gulp. The principal wanted to talk to us? This couldn't be good. We were probably *both* in trouble.

"The vote was very close," Principal Gold continued. "In fact, only ten votes separated the winner from the other candidate. That means neither of you had a real majority, which is why I'd like you to consider working together on the student council. The winner of the election will be president of the sixth grade, and the other girl will be vice president. We've never had a vice president of sixth grade before, but we've never had an election this close before, either."

I looked down at my feet. What the principal was suggesting made sense — or at least it would have if it had been two different girls sitting in her office. But Addie and I working together? That would be impossible. I was pretty sure Addie would feel that way, too.

"I think that's a great idea," Addie chirped in her perky voice.

Okay, I guess I didn't know Addie that well anymore.

"I mean, as long as Jenny doesn't mind being my vice president," Addie continued. "After all, I'd still be in charge, right?"

"Actually, Addie, Jenny is the winner of the election," Principal Gold told her gently. "You would be *her* vice president."

I sat there for a minute in complete shock. Had Principal Gold really said what I thought she'd said. *Jenny is the winner of the election. . . .*

From the look on Addie's face, I was sure I'd heard the principal correctly. It was true. I'd done it! I'd stopped the Pops!

I could hear the cheers through the halls as Principal Gold made the announcement over the loudspeaker. I was standing by my locker, trying to act cool and relaxed about being the winner of the election, but inside I was just bursting. I wanted to scream and yell out that I had beaten Addie Wilson, so loud that they could hear me in China. But that would be bad sportsmanship.

Luckily, I had Chloe to do my screaming for me. I could hear her loud voice over everyone else's in C wing. And a moment later she was by my side, giving me a huge hug.

"You did it! You did it!" she screamed in my ear.

"No, *we* did it. All of us. There's no way I could have won this election without you guys," I told her.

We looked over at Addie, Dana, and Claire. They were all standing by Addie's locker with huge frowns on their faces.

"I'm going to have to work with her, you know," I told Chloe.

Chloe nodded. "That's the bad part. But the good part is you're the boss."

I shrugged. Being the boss wasn't something I was looking forward to. I wasn't very good at telling people what to do.

"So what's your first order of business?" Chloe asked me.

"I have to plan that post-election party," I told her.

"You mean the one for the people who voted for you, right?"

I shook my head. "That's not really right," I told her. "I don't want to be all exclusive and everything. It's gonna be a party for the whole sixth grade. I've already said something to Principal Gold about it. She's going to try and figure out which day we can have the party."

Chloe nodded. "So I guess you'll be pretty busy with that for the next week or so, right?"

I thought about that for a minute. "I'm not a great party planner," I admitted. "But I know someone who is. Come with me."

You should have seen the look on Chloe's face when I dragged her over to Addie's locker.

"What do you want?" Claire demanded.

"Are you here to rub it in?" Dana asked.

I shook my head. "Actually, I'm here to talk to the vice president of the sixth grade class," I explained.

"What do you want?" Addie asked me. She sounded very grouchy. Obviously, she was still mad that she'd lost the election.

"Well, you know that post-election party I talked to Principal Gold about?" I asked her.

Claire laughed. "Oh, great. Jenny McAfee's gonna throw a party."

I shook my head. "Not necessarily," I told her. "I know I'm not very experienced at throwing parties. But Addie is." I turned to Addie. "I thought maybe you'd want to be in charge of this project."

"In charge?" Addie repeated, making sure she'd heard me right.

I nodded. "Just run everything by me before you do it, so I know what's going on."

Addie studied my face. I guess she wanted to make sure this wasn't a prank. But I'd meant what I said. I was delegating. That's a very important thing for a leader to do.

"Wow. Okay. Um, sure," Addie said. "I'll get started today."

"Just remember, it's a party for *everyone*, Addie," I told her.

Addie nodded. "Gotcha."

"Okay, see ya at the student council meeting on Friday," I said. Then I walked off, pulling Chloe away with me.

"Why'd you do that?" Chloe asked as soon as we were out of Addie's earshot.

"I've got more important things to do the rest of this week," I replied.

"Like what? Order the new jukebox or pick a date for field day or . . ."

I shook my head. "I'm going to be helping you get ready for your play audition," I told her. "You need to pick a song and decide on what you're going to wear. And then we need to have you practice in front of an audience – maybe my mom can play the piano."

"Wow. You're gonna do all that for me?" Chloe asked.

"Of course. You helped me win the election, and now I'm going to help you get a great part in the play."

"I really wanted you to win," Chloe said.

"No kidding. I couldn't tell," I teased.

"I guess I went a little overboard as your campaign manager," Chloe said, looking at the ground. "It's just that . . ." She stopped for a minute and sighed.

"Just that what?" I asked her.

"Look, I know what the Pops say about me," Chloe told

me. "About my clothes and how loud I am and all that. They call me a loser all the time. I try to act like it doesn't bother me, but sometimes —"

"But sometimes it gets to you," I said, finishing her sentence. "I know exactly how you feel."

"I just wanted Addie to not be number one for once," Chloe admitted. "Kind of teach her a lesson."

I nodded. I think we'd all felt that way — just not as strongly as Chloe had.

"And I also thought you'd be a great president," Chloe assured me. "You're always thinking about ways to help out other people. Like working with me for the audition. You're a really good friend, Jenny."

"Thanks. So are you," I told her. Then I grabbed her by the arm and dragged her toward the exit. "Now come on. Let's get going. You have a lot of work to do this afternoon."

"You sound like me," Chloe laughed. She paused for a minute. "Do you think Marc will tape me singing so we can all watch it and figure out what I'm doing wrong?"

"Sure he will. Everyone's gonna want to help you," I assured her. "That's what friends are for."

In the Jungle of Middle School, What Animal Are You?

1. **If you could dye your hair any color what would it be?**

   A. Red
   B. Blond
   C. Brown

2. **When you're talking to people, do you**

   A. Touch or poke the person you're talking to?
   B. Stand still with your arms folded in front of you?
   C. Play with your hair, touch your chin, and scratch your nose?

3. When a pal tells a good joke, what's your reaction?

A. Laugh really loudly so everyone hears you.

B. Laugh heartily, but not really loudly.

C. Giggle quietly.

4. When you go to a party, what's your style?

A. Make a grand entrance, just so everyone knows you've arrived.

B. Walk in, look around for someone you know, and go over to say hi.

C. Go inside quietly and head over to a quiet corner.

5. What's your favorite pet?

A. A snake because they're so exciting and different.

B. A dog because they need you to love them, and they love you back.

C. A cat because they don't ask a lot of you.

6. What's your secret passion?

A. Motorcycles

B. Football

C. Writing

What kind of animal are you?

If you answered mostly A's, you are a tigress, an exciting, adventuresome girl who others worship and also fear. You move gracefully through your world, climbing mountains and taking chances. It's important for you to experience everything you can — it's the only way you know to enjoy life.

If you answered mostly B's, you resemble a steady, sturdy tortoise — well, only as far as your personality goes. You take things slow and steady, and are sensible and cautious. Still, you're not overly fearful. In some ways it's as though you have a shell around you, which means you aren't always the easiest to get to know. However, once people take the time to get close to you, they appreciate your good humor and levelheadedness.

If you answered mostly C's, you resemble a gentle, shy lamb. There's a side of you that finds safety in numbers and being part of a crowd. Standing out and making your presence known just isn't your style. You leave center stage for others. You're also incredibly kind. You'd never be the one to hurt someone else's feelings.